It's a gas, gas, gas . . .

Jacques DuBois picked up his beeping cell phone.

"Yeah, Sam," he said gruffly.

"There's been another gas attack in Tokyo."

DuBois brightened. "TALON Force hitting the bricks?"

"You sound up for it," Wong answered.

"Killing killers is my specialty. Cleaning up civilization's mistakes."

"First we have to find them. Every civilized country is sending in relief workers to—"

"TALON Force don't consist of relief workers, Sammy."

Sam sighed. "Well, we're going in *listed* as relief workers, but the Joint Chiefs want us—"

"To kill the killers."

"That about sums it up."

DuBois's hard features slowly split into a predatory grin.

Excellent.

TALON FORCE

HELLSTORM

Cliff Garnett

A SIGNET BOOK

SIGNET
Published by New American Library, a division of
Penguin Putnam Inc., 375 Hudson Street,
New York, New York 10014, U.S.A.
Penguin Books Ltd, 27 Wrights Lane,
London W8 5TZ, England
Penguin Books Australia Ltd, Ringwood,
Victoria, Australia
Penguin Books Canada Ltd, 10 Alcorn Avenue,
Toronto, Ontario, Canada M4V 3B2
Penguin Books (N.Z.) Ltd, 182–190 Wairau Road,
Auckland 10, New Zealand

Penguin Books Ltd, Registered Offices:
Harmondsworth, Middlesex, England

First published by Signet, an imprint of New American Library,
a division of Penguin Putnam Inc.

First Printing, October 2000
10 9 8 7 6 5 4 3 2 1

Copyright © New American Library, 2000
TALON Force is a trademark of Penguin Putnam Inc.

All rights reserved

 REGISTERED TRADEMARK—MARCA REGISTRADA

PUBLISHER'S NOTE
This is a work of fiction. Names, characters, places, and incidents either
are the product of the author's imagination or are used fictitiously,
and any resemblance to actual persons, living or dead, business
establishments, events, or locales is entirely coincidental.

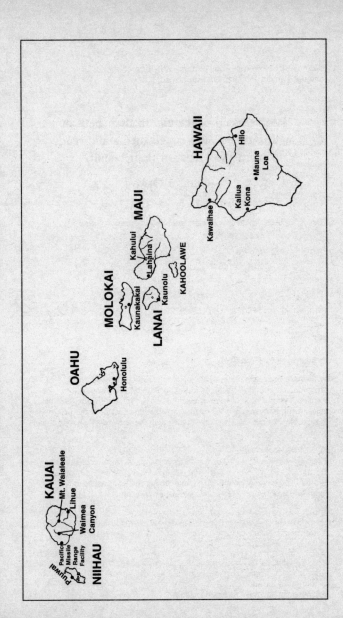

People sleep peacefully in their beds at night only because rough men stand ready to do violence on their behalf.

—George Orwell

Chapter 1

July 18, 1534 hours
Tokyo, Japan

Tatsuko Nakamori ran around the corner in the Ginza and ducked through a crowd of kindergartners out on a stroll. A little boy hit the pavement and started crying. A wrinkled, white-haired principal shouted after him to apologize, but Tatsuko kept running. Then the cops burst through the children, chasing after him.

Ahead, he could hear the under-tumble of the approaching subway train. The entrance was just a hundred feet away. If he could just keep running—and if his lungs didn't explode—he could get down to the platform and leap on the train, then get off at the next stop before the cops could radio ahead.

He leapt the first five steps down into the underground station, grabbing the brass rail to keep from flying headfirst the rest of the way. He thundered on down the steps, but the lead cop was already at the entrance. As Tatsuko hit the platform and sprinted the last few yards toward the open train doors, he glanced behind him to see the cops pouring down the stairs after him. The train shuddered and started to move. Tatsuko reached out to clasp the door just as six short, brutal bomb blasts sent shock waves down the tunnel, deafening commuters.

The tunnel then filled with an invisible gas.

Dozens of people took their hands from their ears and placed them to their throats—and then died. Tatsuko, the cops, the schoolkids—anybody within a block and a half of the blast perished.

Chapter 2

"Travis. It's Sam."

"Yeah, Sam. Go ahead."

"There's a situation in Tokyo. Another Sarin gas attack."

"I thought they had those sons of bitches locked up."

"Could be a copycat. Could be anything at this point."

"I suppose we're going?"

"You got that right, Travis."

Major Travis Beauregard Barrett, U.S. Army, smiled reassuringly at the girl in the tight tennis shorts lying on his scrubby Texas lawn, but his attention was locked on the scrambled cell phone at his ear. "Sam, this would be our first run in a while. Have you actually gotten orders?"

"Well, no, Travis, but they're gonna send us. This is the kind of thing TALON Force was created for."

"*If* it involves American interests. And you'd better pray this signal's secure, Sammy."

"I designed it, Travis," Sam replied testily.

"Then you'd better pray you're as good as you think you are."

"Oh, I am."

"Sam—"

"Hold on a sec." Captain (Temporary) Sam Wong, National Security Agency, twisted away from the brightly lit console to sign the paper the messenger held, then took charge of his delivery. Sam readjusted the headset mike while he opened the package. After a fleeting glance at the sheaf of papers inside, he said to Travis, "*Now* we got orders. The Yakuza sent a message straight to the National Security Agency, saying today was just a test run for an attack on the American embassy."

"The Japanese Mafia? What's in it for them?"

"Let's be sure to ask 'em."

"I'm on my way."

The girl in the tight tennis shorts overheard Travis and smacked her fist into a patch of crabgrass. "Fuck!"

Travis beamed at her with craggy tolerance. Everything about him was craggy, as if he'd been sculpted from granite, but he moved with confident, athletic grave. "That's life in the Green Berets, darlin'."

"Green Berets my ass! I've been comin' onto this post since I was fourteen, and no Green Beret I ever saw carried high-grade communicators."

Travis's smile widened, his tennis hat shadowing the chill in his eyes. "It's a new millennium, Sandra. I got the solar-powered TV"—he gestured at the crisp 15-incher showing TNN videos right beside the net—"I got the five-CD changer and the satellite dish—"

"And a crappy sixty-three Chevy pickup."

"And just about anything that suits my fancy—including you, darlin'." His arm encircled her waist and he pulled her against him. She tried to maintain a pissed-off pout but had to give it up.

"You just got back from that training camp," Sandra whined. "I thought we'd have some quality time together."

"They trained us to do a job. It's the bad guys pick the time when we do it."

Sandra wriggled against his chest. "I know, but I get lonely when you're gone, Trav."

"No more'n me, baby. But I got one wife already—"

"*Ex*-wife."

"Still. I ain't gonna confuse my kids."

"Lotsa guys get married again, Trav. Including guys with kids."

"I ain't lotsa guys."

July 18, 1036 hours
Ellesmere, Greenland

"Stan, it's Sam."

Lieutenant Commander Stanislaus Michael Powczuk, U.S. Navy SEAL, came to a halt in a blue world, thirty feet below pale Arctic ice. His muscular shoulders, almost as wide as he was tall at five-foot-nine, stopped pulling him through a world few men had ever seen, or cared to see. His heartbeat thundered in his ears, but so did the voice from the earplug transceiver he was required to carry when he was away from his cell phone. The satellite communications system worked, even down here. He had to hand it to Sam; the guy was a fucking technological genius.

Stan grunted, and turned to swim back toward the hole he'd come in by, one hundred feet behind him.

"Underwater, huh? Can't talk 'cause your mouth's sucking an air hose till you come up?"

"Hnnn."

"So have I told you about me and Angela? I've always had a thing for tall, stacked women, and there she is! As soon as you headed north, I was over at your place, big guy. She was wearing something small and white, but only for a while—you've probably never even seen it—"

"Sam, my wife would take one look at your sorry skinny ass and fall down laughing."

"Oh, hi, Stan. That was quick."

"As any woman you actually *do* lay says."

" 'Stan, that was quick'? Well, if you hadn't taught 'em to think that was the norm—"

"Sam, is this about the force? Are we out of the blocks?"

"Ah." All of a sudden Sam's voice was subdued.

"Sam?"

"Sorry, buddy—I sort of forgot about a thousand dead people there for a moment."

"A thousand?" When Sam didn't answer, Stan continued, "If they're dead we can avenge 'em but we can't worry about 'em. You gotta look ahead instead of behind you. Give me the details."

As Sam explained the situation, Stan took in every word. Then he thrust himself out of the ice hole into an Arctic snowstorm, the seawater surging around him. He pulled his tank and flippers off, then began a dead run toward base camp in his scuba boots. "On my way!" he shouted to the skies.

Damn, life is good.

July 18, 1143 hours
Brazil

"Sarah. Sam."

Captain Sarah Greene, U. S. Army, was on her knees in the mud beside an ancient mossy tree in the Amazon rainforest, her short black hair stark against the deep jungle greens. A lichen on that tree had markings she'd never seen before, but judging from the ferns downstream, it as more likely to make a poultice than a poison. Probably very good for blood clotting.

"Sarah? You reading me?"

Her perky nose wrinkled as she fished the cell phone from her rucksack. "What is it, Sam?"

"We've got a mission."

"Really? Or maybe, *naturally*. I'm way the heck down in the middle of nowhere. Where are all the others?"

"Well, Stan's farther north than you are south. But I've only talked with him and Travis."

"Why's that? I'm not third on the chain of command."

"Right. Well, I had to call them first, since they *are* number one and number two. But then I . . . thought you should hear next. I'm sorry, Sarah. You won't like it."

Her heart hit her throat, just once. Then she sat on a banana leaf and said in a very calm voice, "Tell me."

"Another Sarin attack in Tokyo."

Sarah didn't say anything for a good thirty seconds. Sweat slid off her clamped chin and splattered on the leaf. Finally, in a voice even calmer than before, she said, "Can I get a flight out of Jaburu?"

"There'll be a chopper standing by when you get there. It'll take you to Manaus for a jet to Utah."

"I'm on my way. And . . . thank you, Sam."

"For what?"

"For the way you told me."

Sam shrugged uncomfortably. "Hell, Sarah, I don't know what you're talking about."

Sarah Greene stood up and tried a smile, but just couldn't muster it.

July 18, 0851 hours
Grants, New Mexico

"Hunter. This is Sam."

The eyes of Captain Hunter Evans Blake III, U.S.

Air Force, narrowed behind his shades. Ahead lay the vast expanse of his ranch in the New Mexican mountains; colorful, rugged, and two thousand feet below. He had been drinking it in from his gossamer-red ultralight, surrounded by nothing but the empty moan of the wind. But when he heard Sam's voice in his flight helmet, he switched off the stunning beauty like bad TV.

"Hunter here."

"The Yakuza just killed a thousand people in Tokyo with Sarin gas."

The crisp, pure mountain air filled Hunter's lungs. "Indiscriminate murder of civilians, huh?" The ultralight hit downdraft and Hunter automatically compensated for the change in air pressure. "Cold-blooded murder. It seems like it's happening more and more. Somalia, Bosnia, Kosovo, East Timor . . . remember when there were rules to war?"

"Well, no, actually. I'm not career military like the rest of you. But I know what you're saying."

"I think we're in an era when big wars between big powers are unthinkable, so all the little guys who used to pick a side and stand on the sidelines cheering us big guys on have no place to put their energy. More than that, since they were just cheerleaders, they have no experience with playing the game."

"So you're saying the defeat of the Soviets was a bad thing?"

"Every action has consequences, and some are unintended."

"You're a true philosopher, Hunter."

"I spend a lot of time hovering above the world. Gives a man time to think. But consequences have consequences, too. That's why they created TALON Force, right? You're about to see firsthand what happens to guys who gas civilians." He shifted the ultralight's controls and began his long, quick descent.

July 18, 1102 hours
New York, New York

"Hey, Jen. Sam here."

Lieutenant Jennifer Margaret Olsen, U.S. Navy, burst out laughing. Here she was standing in the middle of New York's Saks Fifth Avenue, being addressed as "Mrs. Jayne Weatherford Breckinridge," and then her purse starts talking. "A moment, if you please, dear," she said to the saleswoman, and waved her away in dismissal.

Jennifer walked across the polished floor toward an untenanted display of kitchen aprons. Five hundred dollar aprons, mind you, but still not the thing to draw Manhattan socialites in droves. What *was* the manufacturer thinking?

"Okay, Sam, I've got some privacy, but make it quick."

"Gee, I guess that *is* what they say."

"What? I didn't catch that."

"Jen, there's been a Sarin attack in Tokyo. This isn't really your department, but the way I see it—"

"Sam, I wouldn't miss a mission for anything. You know that."

"I mean, there's no obvious need for espionage, let alone intel ops—"

"Then I'll gaze adoringly at the rest of you."

Sam burst out laughing. "As if!"

"Thanks, Sam. See you there."

Jennifer dropped the satellite clip back in her purse. For a moment an observer might have seen a beautiful, buxom young woman, her blonde hair straining against the bun it found itself in at the moment—but the next moment he'd have seen a gracefully aging matron from East Sixty-sixth strolling back to the silks department. In a voice a full octave lower than the voice Sam heard on the phone, she said to the saleswoman, "Dear me, I'm afraid I forgot a board meeting at the Metropolitan."

"Opera?"

"Museum."

"Oh, of course, Mrs. Breckinridge."

"Thank you so much for all your help."

"My pleasure."

Jennifer walked with haughty reserve out the front door. After a block, she ducked down an alley. At the far end her hair was free and her swinging hips were drawing all eyes.

Punching the next button on his blinking console, Sam's mind's eye could imagine it all.

July 18, 0811 hours
Twentynine Palms, California

"One fifteen—one sixteen—"

"Jack. It's Sambo."

Captain Jacques Henri DuBois, U. S. Marine Corps, came to a halt, held two feet from the floor solely by his left arm. The crowd of young Marines around him urged him on. "Keep going, sir!"

He gave his head a short, negative shake as he swung his feet around in front of him, still holding himself up by the one arm. If Travis looked like he was carved from rock, Jack looked like he was carved from God's own bicep. He lowered himself to his butt and looked around with assured command. "No more push-ups today, guys. Time to do some bidness."

With mutterings of disappointment and awe, the young Marines went from Jack's spartan quarters into the harsh desert glare of the Marine Corps Air-Ground Combat Center at Twentynine Palms, California. As the door closed behind them, he picked up a cell phone and spoke again.

"Yeah, Sam?"

"Another gas attack in Tokyo."

"And TALON Force hits the bricks?"

"*You* sound up for it."

"Killing killers is my specialty. Cleaning up civilization's mistakes."

"Well, we've got killers. The Yakuza—"

"The Japanese Mafia?" Jack's savage grin seemed almost audible to Sam along the open line.

Sam nodded, uplit by his console blinking lights. "That about sums it up."

Chapter 3

July 18, 1415 hours
Crow Basin, Utah

Once there was a secret base in the Nevada desert called Area 51, or Dreamland, or Groom Lake. The problem was, it didn't stay secret for long. After many years of denying the existence of a place that everybody knew full well existed, the U.S. military moved its black ops to two bases in more military-friendly Utah. One is on land adjacent to the old Dugway Proving Grounds, the onetime home of nerve and biological warfare studies. But the *real* operations take place at the second base on the other side of the state, in the misleadingly named Sweet Water Canyon. It's an area far from any main road, reachable only by increasingly poor dirt tracks that tend to fork again and again until a casual explorer has no idea where he's going or where he came from.

It was at this second base, known as Crow Basin, where the members of TALON Force Eagle Team were ordered to converge for briefing.

One by one, the seven members of Eagle Team arrived. Travis, coming from Texas, actually beat Hunter from New Mexico and Jack from California, but that was just like Travis; he didn't become TALON's leader by being second. Jen, out of New York, and Sam from Washington, D.C., were the next to arrive.

Stan was due from the North Pole at 1530, and Sarah would show up from South America just afterward.

Sam Wong stood looking at the mountains off in the distance, looming like multihued giants in the pink of dusk. Utah was a great place for rocks. Though it was an awesome spectacle, Sam was not impressed. You've seen one rock, you've seen 'em all, was his thinking. Besides, Sam felt more comfortable in a cubicle with a computer and a Mountain Dew, and didn't need the grandeur of the great outdoors. Bored with the sights, he strolled over to the C–117 Globemaster that would transport the team to Japan, showed his ID to the guards, and went inside to inspect the team's gear.

Meanwhile, Jack DuBois was out in the multicolored desert, killing time by killing rattlers with a stick.

It was something he'd gotten into since he'd been based out west in Twentynine Palms. He'd enjoyed it so much that he started doing it when he went home to Georgia, too. And those mountain rattlers were mean. Compared to them, these desert snakes were pussycats.

To Travis, who was watching him from a distance, it was the damnedest thing he'd ever seen.

Jack would creep across the desert carrying a brown cloth bag of rattlers. He'd explained to Travis that snakes could sense the vibrations of approaching footsteps so a hunter had to walk softly, but they couldn't make any sense of the sound of other rattles. Jack would come upon one of them, four feet long and as thick around as his wrist, spread across a rock or curled up on a patch of sand. The snake, surprised to see him but finding that he made no hostile moves, held its ground—prepared to fight if necessary, but remaining wary. That was when Jack would squat down about two feet away and reach out to it with a sturdy, black, twisted stick he'd picked up as he'd left the occupied area of the base. He would slide the stick under the snake's belly and lift. The snake would calmly accept the boost; it would hang poised over the stick, ready as ever. Until he slid it in the bag.

"You're not gonna tell me those things taste like chicken, are you?" Travis asked him.

"*Everything* tastes like chicken, Travis. Don't you know that? Gator does. People, too, they tell me," Jack answered. "That's why I eat beef."

"So you're not gonna eat those ol' boys?"

"Hell, no. When we're ready to take off I'll turn 'em loose."

"Aren't you gonna leave a lotta pissed-off rattlers right near the base?"

"It's good practice for the personnel, man. That's what *I* do it for: practice. Hand-eye coordination, coolness under pressure."

"How much pressure is there, really?"

"You try it."

"No, I'm just asking, thanks. But it looks like those snakes are sleepy from the sun. Is this one of those deals where you're really in no danger at all?"

Jack considered him. "Well, let's go see."

He picked up his hissing bag and crept toward the mountains, Travis following close behind. Soon he stopped, set the bag down, and motioned for Travis to come forward. Travis stopped five feet away to watch Jack, two feet away from the biggest rattler he'd ever seen. He couldn't tell how long it was because it was coiled on a flat rock with two other rocks forming a low wall behind it. But it was as thick as a loaf of bread.

"Now," said Jack, "this guy's got the rock and the reflected heat from the other rocks, so he's about as baked as he can be." Jack reached out with his stick, exactly as he had the other times Travis had seen him.

But the rattler struck at Jack's hand as he drove the stick in its face.

Before Travis could recoil, Jack had the snake pinned to the rock, the stick tight against its thick neck. The nearly six-foot reptile writhed and flapped against the stone, its powerful muscles rippling in the sunlight, its tail rattling furiously.

"This one's a killer," said Jack. "He got big and old and mean."

With one thrust he drove the blunt stick through the snake's neck. It wasn't clean but it was brutally effective. Its blood spread across the surface of the rock, filling the dry air with a coppery scent. As the rattler died it kept on flopping, whipping its body in increasingly slower movements until it finally lay still.

"What tipped you that the snake was gonna strike?" Travis asked.

"There are signs."

"But your hand kept moving forward."

"That's the test, isn't it?"

"For you, maybe. Me, I'd rather patrol Bosnia." Which he had done, as well as Somalia and Iraq. There was nothing human that could scare Travis Barrett, but he, like Indiana Jones and anybody with the sense God gave a goose, he thought, had a thing about snakes. "I'd rather come out here with a double-ought and blow those bastards to little pieces."

"Now that's where your Texas upbringing—" Jack stopped. He'd heard something, and so had Travis. The two men stood motionless in the afternoon sun and let the wind carry whatever sound they had heard back to them once more.

They soon heard the noise again—small rocks clattering down a stone wall, in the colorful arroyo fifty yards to the east.

Travis and Jack both crept toward the sound as one, Jack leaving his hissing bag behind. They reached the arroyo where multicolored stone shot up from the earth, beginning the rise that would eventually stretch out into a long ridge in the distance. There was a cleft in the rock just wide enough to afford purchase. Jack and Travis climbed up the rock facing, one on either side of the cleft, using the various outcroppings to pull themselves along.

The rock was searing hot, and there were many loose pebbles. Travis and Jack used their years of recon and Special Forces training to pass the pebbles by without disturbing them—as someone else had apparently not been able to do. After climbing fifteen feet up the sloping stone they moved a little closer to the top of the cleft, keeping each other in sight while making sure they were able to look down into the opening.

Thirty seconds later they came upon two young men walking and climbing their way toward the desert.

"This is so cool!" whispered the blond one, who looked to be about twenty.

"My brother sneaked up on Area 51 back before the Army took White Sides," said the dark-haired one, who looked to be the same age but whose hair was already thinning. "But that was nothing compared to—"

Suddenly his feet flew out from under him as he tried to jump backward. In a blink, Jack was standing in front of him, his Tanto knife catching sunlight in one hand.

"Hey! What the—?" stammered the dark-haired one from his back.

"What country is this?" asked Jack, his flat voice echoing in the cleft.

"What?"

"What country?"

"It's—it's America," said the blond guy. "Land of the free!"

"Also the land of high literacy rates," Jack said. "So I assume you guys can read the signs posted all over the other side of the mountain. You know, the ones that say 'Restricted Area, No Trespassing.' And 'Use of Deadly Force Authorized.' "

"But this—this is a free country!" said the blond guy urgently.

"But not an anarchy. A country has laws. Break the

law, you pay the price." Jack started to crowd toward the guy.

"We, we didn't mean any harm!" said the other one. "We just wanted to—to *do* it! To get in and out! To say that we did! To—"

"I get your story," said Jack. "What I don't get is why I should care. This base is restricted for a reason, and a whole lot more than your two lives depends on its staying that way. You knew the penalty when you came in—"

"That'll do, Captain," said Travis from where he'd maneuvered behind the two young men without making a sound. He was not going to use a given name in this situation.

"But Major, this is clear—"

"That'll do." Travis stepped beside Jack, and spoke to the kids. "Gentlemen, my friend is not kidding you. He believes in the law, and the law he most believes in is the law of Moses: 'an eye for an eye and a tooth for a tooth.' You're in the middle of empty country in violation of all law. You can't be seen from any direction but up. Who's gonna know what happens out here?"

"We're—we're sorry . . ." stammered the dark-haired youth.

"And you'll be sorrier once you pay the seven hundred and fifty dollar fine—each."

"Seven hundred and fifty dollars?!"

"That's the posted, authorized fine."

"You can explain it all to security," said Travis. "They'll be here in two minutes to escort you back to your vehicle and get all the information to process your fines."

Chapter 4

The C-117 Globemaster lifted off from Crow Basin two minutes after Sarah's jet arrived from South America. Master Sergeant McKenna's men had her and her baggage transferred in one smooth motion; the rest of her gear was already on board. As the C-117, known as the "Cadillac of transports," rose above the anonymous Utah desert, it turned for a run straight toward the setting sun.

"Hi, Sarah."

"Hi, Stan. Guys."

"Your knees are dirty," Sam pointed out.

"Gosh, I didn't even notice."

"From homeopathic medicine to nerve gas," said Travis. "That's quite a jump."

"There was a beautiful lichen . . ."

The banter continued, but Hunter shut it out and studied the others. It had been months since he had seen them all, but now that they were together, it was like they were never apart.

Travis Barrett always looked like a recruiting ad, Hunter mused. Not one brush-cut hair was out of place, his pleats were razor-sharp, his Green Beret's green beret cleaned and ironed, and he was buff *almost* beyond belief after three hundred push-ups every day.

Almost—because Jack DuBois had three inches and thirty pounds on Travis's six-two two hundred, and Jack could do five hundred push-ups with each arm. Hunter had seen him do it once, and while he was cranking out reps, Jack calmly read *The Art of War.* Jack had his softer side. He had a dog and played a mean drum, specializing in jazz and rock—but Hunter knew that when push came to shove, Jack could be stone-cold crazy.

Everyone on TALON Force had his own rough edge sometimes. But Jack was ready to go 24/7, as two blind or just plain stupid muggers learned last April. If Jack hadn't had friends in *really* high places . . .

People like Travis and Jack were born ready. And so was Stan, Hunter continued to reflect. At five-foot-nine, Stan Powczuk had the Napoleonic need to be the toughest bastard in the room. Problem was, Hunter didn't back down to anybody, either. Whenever they were together, they ended up in each other's faces sooner rather than later. If they both didn't put the mission ahead of the man, somebody would have long since ended up in the hospital, because Stan was a veritable pit bull.

Sam . . . was Sam. He looked like a geek, until you saw how wiry his arms were. During their original training, he'd put every bit of muscle he could on his five-six frame. And if it still left him a physical lightweight on the team, that was okay, because he was the outright mental champ. Sam was the point man of every plan. He was so smart he usually knew what the Joint Chiefs were planning even before they did. To him, TALON Force was a video game times ten.

Finally, there were the women—who couldn't have been more different. Jen was a born actress. She was beautiful, she was talented, and she gave up what could have been a lucrative career in Vegas or Hollywood—but she wanted to do this.

Sarah, who was now turning toward the front of the

cabin, was the only one Hunter had really worried about at the start. But she'd done everything the Chiefs asked of her, even though she was just a five-four pixie. With freckles and green eyes, she was also the best damn doctor Hunter had ever seen, and he'd had occasion to see a few. It wasn't her fault that her mom had been a hippie, but she seemed to have overcome her initial crunchy upbringing and had proven herself every bit a warrior during their last mission.

Meanwhile, Stan watched Hunter watch the others. Hunter liked to stand apart from the crowd and watch. Either that trait had drawn him to piloting, or piloting had brought out that trait in him. Either way, Stan thought he often saw himself above and apart from the team—looking down. It made him aloof and mysterious, catnip for the ladies. It also made him an asshole as far as Stan was concerned. And then, of course, Hunter was the only son of a high-ranking Air Force general and some rich bitch, while Stan's dad was an Aliquippa, PA steel worker, killed when Stan was a kid. They had to work together because the Joint Chiefs had picked them for TALON along with the others. They had got along all right for the most part, but they were never going to be best friends.

Travis strode to the front of the transport's briefing area.

"Ladies. Gentlemen. As Sam has informed you, a threat has been made against the American embassy in Tokyo, and due to the circumstances of the last twenty-four hours, the Joint Chiefs are taking that threat extremely seriously. General Krauss has informed me that a member of the Japanese military, Major Yuki Kurimoto, had been working to infiltrate the Yakuza before this event occurred. Major Kurimoto will brief us on arrival, and his assessment of the situation will play a part in my decision on how to proceed. But I will, naturally, do what I think is best for our interests."

"Right on!" shouted Stan.

"That'll do, cowboy," drawled Travis. "We spent a week in January refreshing our skills regarding attacks by gas and nerve agents. I would expect you all to remember what was said, but to be safe I've asked Sarah to give us a refresher course as we cross the Pacific."

Sarah stuck a folded reddish leaf she'd brought from the Amazon between her cheek and her gum, in order to counteract all the jet lag she was experiencing, then rapped on the front wall. When she had everyone's attention she smiled her lopsided smile, made particularly lopsided by the leaf. "Hi, everybody. Hope you've all been well since our last get-together."

The others smiled back, but they'd just as soon skip the preliminaries. They wanted to know what they'd need to know. Still, this was her area of expertise, the reason she was here, and she'd do her job the way *she* thought best.

She pushed a button in the wall and a slide was protected from the far wall to the area beside her head. She took a moment to marvel at the military's efficiency: she had prepared slides for this scenario a long time ago, having handed them over to Brigadier General Jack Krauss over a year ago, and now, when she needed them, they were here, updated to the minute. That was the level of competence and commitment on TALON Force, and that was impressive.

The slide showed something like a scene from a bad movie: men, women, and children lying haphazardly on a Tokyo street. You half expected Godzilla to stomp by any minute. She turned and pointed at the picture with two outstretched fingers.

"On March 20, 1995, the Aum Shinri Kyo cult set off a Sarin attack in a Tokyo subway. They'd brewed the gas in a bathtub and given their general level of competence, their gas killed *only* eleven people, while injuring fifty-five hundred. I was there, and the effects were devastating, both physiologically and ecologically."

"There she goes again with that granola stuff," quipped Stan.

Sarah shot him a dirty look and continued. "The Sarin in the new attack was dispersed far more effectively. As of seventeen minutes ago, eleven hundred ninety-two people were dead, and there are more to come."

"But these bombs went off in the subway, too," interjected Travis. "Wouldn't that have contained the gas underground like before?"

"This time they set off six bombs, each beside an entrance or an air vent. They could certainly have killed more people if they'd planted them outside on the street, but they probably wanted to induce the panic that comes from hiding them underground. You *might* spot a bomb on the street, but you *never* know what's under your feet."

"Got it," said Travis.

"If a bomb is detonated inside the American embassy, it might not kill everyone because of the enclosed environment, but that would be a small comfort. Such a bomb would certainly be placed to kill as many as possible, and even one death by Sarin. . . ."

Sarah took a deep breath. "Sarin, a colorless and odorless nerve agent, has a lethal dose of point-five milligram for an adult. That's twenty-six times deadlier than cyanide gas. The vapor is slightly heavier than air. Under wet and humid weather conditions it degrades swiftly, but as the temperature rises, its lethal duration increases, despite the humidity.

"Nerve agents, so called because they affect the transmission of nerve impulses, can be manufactured by means of fairly simple chemical techniques. The raw materials are cheap and generally available. Major symptoms include contraction of the pupils, blurred vision, ocular pain, headache, difficulty breathing, coughing, nausea, vomiting, muscle weakness, and agitation.

In the absence of treatment, death is caused through suffocating resulting from airway obstruction by excessive bronchial secretions and weakness of the respiratory muscles. With assisted ventilation and clearing of the airway, an individual may survive several doses of a nerve agent—but you wouldn't want to try it."

She punched the button and another picture appeared, this time of a Nazi chemical lab.

"Nerve agents have entirely dominated warfare since World War Two. Sarin was created by the Germans in 1938. During the war two more agents, Tabun and Soman, were created. Widespread use of these agents could have easily won the war for Germany, but Hitler halted their production. His minister of production, Albert Speer, said later, 'All sensible army people turned gas warfare down as being utterly insane, since, in view of America's superiority in the air, it would not be long before it would bring the most terrible catastrophe upon German cities.'

"In the Iran-Iraq war in the eighties, Saddam Hussein used Tabun and other nerve agents against Iran. Then we had the Aum Shinri Kyo cult. An often-missed fact about Aum Shinri Kyo is that its membership extended beyond Japan. There were thirty thousand members in Russia, as well. It is still a viable threat."

"So where does the Yakuza come into the picture?" asked Jennifer.

"Unknown, so far," said Sarah. "But they're notorious for finding a way into anything if the money's right."

"There's no money in bombing an embassy," said Hunter.

"A venerable sage was once asked the meaning of life, Hunter," answered Sarah. "He said, 'I don't know, man; I didn't do it.'" A ripple of laughter ran through the room. "I can only tell you what I can tell you," she continued. "Now pay attention. Your lives may depend on this information."

A new slide appeared, divided horizontally and vertically. "There are four cornerstones in the protection against nerve agents. The more of them in place, the better your chances for survival. These are one, physical protection, two, medical protection, three, early detection, and four, decontamination.

"Physical protection consists of body and respiratory protection, in the form of a decontamination suit. Medical protection can be provided pretreatment with drugs to minimize the effects of the agent. Canada has developed a mixture of potassium two, three-butadion monoximate, which can be applied beforehand as a protective cream. This is not yet a science; there were still severe effects suffered by many soldiers after the Gulf War, despite the cream.

"The decontamination suit—in the case a Level A—consists of a protective mask, protective all-enveloping clothing, boots, and gloves, as well as an individual decontamination kit with medical antidotes. The kit contains a mixture of chlorinated lime and magnesium oxide. This decontaminant works by absorbing liquid substances and also by releasing free chlorine, which has a destructive effect on Sarin. The dry powder also has proven effects on thickened agents, since it cakes together the sticky substance and makes it easier to remove. On the other hand, chlorinated lime has an irritating effect on the skin, so comprehensive use should be followed by a shower or bath within a few hours. We used to use liquid decontaminants—sodium phenolate or sodium cresolate in an alcohol solution—but the dry method has better results.

"If you suspect your skin has been exposed to Sarin and you're unable to use the prepared protection, you must decontaminate within one minute. All our experience says the most important factor is time; the means used is almost irrelevant. You can get good results with soap and water, talcum powder, or even flour. Organized disaster sites now include portable showers. But there may be particular problems when caring for the injured since you may have to remove their clothes. This must be done in such a way that the patient is not injured by more contact with the nerve agent.

"Training in how to behave in chemical warfare protective equipment is essential. Even though you have been thoroughly trained, and have access to the best possible protective equipment, there will be a decrease in your performance if exposed to an agent. It is easy to become overheated. Protective equipment is relatively clumsy, which results in most tasks taking longer to perform than ordinarily. Endurance decreases and it becomes difficult to communicate with others.

"That's all I have to say. I'd advise you to review these specific procedures as we wing our way to beautiful downtown Tokyo." Sarah's voice suddenly broke at the mention of the city. She smiled, trying to cover it. She lowered her eyes as if she were reviewing her notes, but what she saw was memory . . .

Chapter 5

"*He* wants to see you, Lieutenant."

Sarah Greene—a younger Sarah Greene—glanced up from her *New England Journal of Medicine* at Major Danning, standing in the aisle.

"*He?*" she asked.

"That's affirmative."

She jumped up, spilling her cinnamon tea and splashing her left leg; fortunately it had grown cold while she was engrossed in the *Journal*. "I'll just, um, make a stop in the ladies' room," she said, bending to wipe her leg with her hand as she followed Danning down the aisle. He said nothing, but a grin played across his face.

Two minutes later, tea droplets still shining on her ankle, Lieutenant Greene was ushered into the commander's compartment at the back of the transport plane. She saluted, reported, and stood really straight.

"At ease, Lieutenant."

"Yes, sir." Now she just stood straight.

"You know who I am." It was not a question.

"Yes, sir, General Krauss."

"I've been wanting to meet you, Lieutenant."

"Me, sir?"

"Yes. I had planned to drop by while I was in Germany, since you were stationed at Rhein-Main, but fate, it seems, has put us both on this long flight to Tokyo."

"Yes, sir."

"Sit down, Lieutenant. I'm afraid you're going to hurt something, standing like that."

Gratefully, Sarah sat on one of the cushioned chairs facing the general. Since she was only 5'4", she had to place her butt right on the front edge of the seat in order to get her feet all the way to the floor.

General Jack Krauss, Commander-in-Chief, Atlantic Forces, looked through a file he held. "Sarah Greene. No middle name."

"My parents didn't believe in them, sir. Steve Allen—you know Steve Allen, the comedian and author—told a story once . . ." Her voice ran down as she realized she was babbling.

"Go on."

"Are . . . you sure you want to hear this, sir?"

"I'll know when you get done, won't I?"

"Yes, sir. Well, sir, when one of Steve Allen's sons was born, he had to fill out a hospital form, and it asked for a middle name, and he didn't want to give his son one, so he wrote 'None.' Then he thought, maybe they'll think *that's* his middle name, so he put parentheses around it." She drew the curves in the air with her hands. "So when he got the official birth certificate, it listed the middle name as 'Wonel.' Like, a parenthesis and an 'N' together look like a 'W,' and then the other . . ." *Oh God! What was she talking about?*

"But your parents got around that problem. You're not 'Wonel' or anything."

"No, sir."

"I imagine unconventional names were not so unconventional where you grew up."

"Well, sir, Vermont is a funny place. If you're born there, like me and my dad, you're a Vermonter forever. My mom came from Boston, and even though she's lived there over thirty years, she'll always be an outsider."

"Clannish."

"Yes, sir. Vermonters think it's weird when a Vermonter leaves Vermont. Like, when I went to West Point—"

"That's what I'm wondering about, Lieutenant. You went to West Point, but your outsider mom from Boston was, for want of a better term, a hippie."

"Well, yes, sir. But she didn't name me Rainbow or Sunflower. She just wasn't into middle names."

"I'm not trying to impugn your mother. I'm just wondering how she felt when you decided to join the Army."

"It surprised her, sir. That's true. But my parents raised me to stand up for what I believe, and they respected my decision."

"Just why did you make that decision, Lieutenant?"

"Vermont is a funny place, sir. There is still, and probably always has been, something akin to a hippie ethic there—living on the land, respecting nature—"

"Drugs."

"I wouldn't know, sir."

"Don't bullshit me, Lieutenant. Are you telling me you've never had a toke?"

"Uh, um, yes, sir."

"You know, Lieutenant, I would hate to think that any of my officers was lying to me. And I might note, in passing, that we're somewhere over Russian air space, outside the DEA's jurisdiction."

"And *inside* an American military aircraft, sir."

"That's so. Well, what's your opinion of cocaine?"

"I'm against it, sir. It damages the brain."

"And heroin?"

"*God*, no!" She stood up. "Sir, am I under investigation for something?"

"Not in any sense you mean, Lieutenant. Sit down. I'm just trying to get a better picture of you."

"If it's the earrings I wear off duty, sir. I know there

are five of them, but they're just clip-on. And—and I'm entitled to a private life. . . ."

He waited her out. "Now, you were telling me about Vermont, and West Point."

She sat silent for a moment, indecisive. "Yes, sir. Vermont has a hippie ethic—with or without drugs— but it also has a conservative ethic. Maybe I should say 'libertarian.' You don't get a very red neck that far north. And my dad is a veterinarian, as I guess you know. Vets can't be sentenced to HMOs like regular doctors—they *have* to go out and visit their patients on the farms. So I put all that together my own way and decided I could help people, all around the world, by being a doctor in a force that goes everywhere."

"Would you kill someone?"

"As a doctor?"

"As a combatant. Say, if you'd served in Desert Storm and been pinned down with your unit."

"Um . . . yes, sir."

"You're not sure."

"Well, I'd prefer not to, sir. But if it was a question of saving lives in my unit, I would. I've been fully trained to do so, of course."

"You have qualms."

"Sir, could you please tell me why you're asking these questions? I admit you have a wonderful bedside manner, you can make people, me, very comfortable. But I'm a junior officer—"

"You have my permission to speak freely, Lieutenant. Nothing you say will leave this compartment, or enter any official record. I give you my word on it."

"Then—yes, sir, I would kill if I had to. But I hope it never comes to that."

"Don't we all. But unfortunately, sometimes it does."

"I know." She smiled her rueful gamin smile. "Now you see the two Vermonts in me."

"I do."

"But sir, you haven't told me why you're asking these questions . . . ?"

"Oh, just a little project I'm working on."

"I didn't make the cut, did I?"

He smiled. "I'm afraid not."

"Because I don't like killing?"

"Very few people like killing."

"But that's it, isn't it? My . . . 'qualms.' "

"I wouldn't worry about it, Lieutenant. Very few people are going to make my cut. But I was certainly dazzled by your record. A doctor who has received glowing reports from all her superiors, up and down the line. A doctor who is a board-certified surgeon and a microbiologist. An expert at infectious diseases and bio-weapons. And at such a young age."

"Well, that's what I'm really cut out for, sir. That's why I'm here—now that terrorists have attacked the Tokyo subway with Sarin gas."

Chapter 6

The transport hit the tarmac just after two p.m. Tokyo time. It rolled down the outermost runway at Yokota Air Force Base without slowing any more than necessary, until it entered the outermost hangar. Doors five stories high rolled closed behind them. When TALON Force left the aircraft, there was only one man there to meet them—a Japanese with short-cut hair and a fully buttoned trench coat, despite the sweltering summer heat. He had the saddest face Travis had ever seen, with massive bags under his eyes. But when he spoke it was pure military precision.

"Major Yuki Kurimoto," the man introduced himself, stepping forward smartly and saluting.

Travis returned the salute on behalf of his team. "Good to meet you, Major." He introduced the others. Kurimoto looked each over carefully, seemingly keeping a few opinions to himself.

"Problem, Major?" Travis asked with craggy pleasantry.

"Not at all, Major Barrett. It is simply that your dossiers—even the name of your unit—are a closely held secret. I have been permitted to know that secret, and I am duly impressed. So I am interested in the people behind the names." He gave a slight, pro forma smile, barely moving his muscles. "And, of course, it remains one of the glories of the Western world to create a team of mixed genders and multiple races."

"Yeah, we stand for universal brotherhood," said Stan. "Now, what do you have for us to work on?"

Kurimoto's welcoming smile went away. "You realize, Lieutenant Powczuk, that you are here to assist our country."

"Of course I do, Major," said Stan. "But we're the best damn assisters you're going to find."

Hunter smiled engagingly. "What my colleague means—"

"He knows what I mean, Hunter!" Stan snapped.

Kurimoto stepped back. "I know that you seven theoretically compose the cream of the U.S. military."

"There ain't no 'theoretical' about it, Kurimoto-san," said Stan.

The Japanese bowed his head slightly, acknowledging the remark but not necessarily agreeing. "You were assembled by the Joint Chiefs of Staff and receive your orders from one of them on a rotating basis. Supposedly, you are so good that if one of you is captured, the U.S. will spare no efforts to rescue you, because that's more effective than replacing you."

"That's not good enough for you?" asked Stan.

"No," said Kurimoto. "I know American culture. Rank and reputation aren't necessarily earned. I will wait until I see you in action."

"Which is what we want from you," said Hunter. "Action." It was one thing if someone within the chain of command had questions about his teammates, but quite another from an outsider.

"We're all on the same side here," said Travis, in a tone that effectively told them all that this discussion was at an end. "Our enemy is the group that detonated the bombs. So, Major, what do you have on the Yakuza?"

"Nothing yet, I'm sorry to say. Despite the most strenuous efforts," Kurimoto felt compelled to add.

"But I expect to have something this very evening. There is an extraordinary meeting of the Yakuza, and I will be in attendance."

Jack said, "I thought the Yakuza was too tightly knit to infiltrate. Don't they have tattoos, and cut off . . ."

Kurimoto raised his right hand. The top joint of the little finger was missing. "I have been a *wakashu* in the *Yamaguchi-gumi* for three years," he said. "This isolated hangar is not only to conceal *your* identity."

"Now I know what the raincoat's all about," said Jen.

"The *Yamaguchi-gumi* is the highest-ranking clan," Sam explained to his teammates. "All clans operate as 'families,' with the bosses called 'fathers.' The hierarchy moves down from there, with 'uncles,' 'brothers,' 'younger brothers,' 'sons' . . . 'Wakashu' means 'son.' "

"I'm just a cog in the wheel—able to be around without attracting much attention," said Kurimoto.

"But you have to do the dirty work sometimes," said Jen shrewdly.

"I've killed on their behalf, yes. The victim was a man law enforcement had no use for, either, if that's any excuse. But I had to do it to maintain my cover. Even so, I was just sloppy enough that they disciplined me"—again, Kurimoto showed his missing joint—"and assigned me to strong-arm work—the *gurentai*—so I won't be asked to kill again."

"How are you supposed to beat on people if they screw with your hands?" asked Travis.

"The name 'Ya-ku-za' means 'eight-nine-three,' the worst hand in *hanafuda*, a card game much like your blackjack. 'Yakuza' meant 'useless hand' in cards, and then came to mean 'useless hand' in the sense of a hand on a ship or a ranch—a misfit in society. But over time, the actual hand became a symbol of membership. 'Screwing with the hand' was a mark of a mistake."

"So the Yakuza kill without compunction," said
Sarah.

Kurimoto grimaced. "That's what confuses me," he
said. "The Yakuza don't kill indiscriminately. It is part
of their honor. I'm not at all certain that this threat
against your embassy actually came from them. But if
not, I expect they know who did, or will know after
tonight."

Sam nodded. "All right. That's a good start. Jen
and I will be your backup."

Now Kurimoto looked annoyed. "You act as if you
understand the Yakuza, Captain Wong."

"I do. I've done substantial research on the Net.
Besides, I speak Japanese, and Jen's our master of
disguise. We won't blow your cover."

"You're right, you will not. This is a one-man operation. May I respectfully remind you—"

"Yeah, yeah. This is not our country. We haven't
forgotten," said Sam. "But what if that one man
doesn't come back? Then we won't know anything."

Jen said, "It's safer with three of us, really. We can't
afford to fall any further behind the bombers." She
turned a dazzling smile on him. "Let me do the
makeup, then you tell me if we pass muster."

But Kurimoto wasn't quite so easily won. "Do *you*
speak Japanese?"

"You know our culture, and I know the Yakuza's"
she answered sweetly. "I'm a woman; I'm not supposed to talk."

Chapter 7

The lights in the Asakusa district were bright as the three young Japanese strode along the thoroughfare. The two men were typical Yakuza—flashy suits, short hair, wearing dark glasses even at night. Just peeking out from above their collars and beyond their cuffs were elaborate tattoos—tattoos that theoretically ran from their necks to their wrists and calves. The skinny one looked as if he might have had a Chinese mother somewhere in his family tree, but also looked like he'd kill you if you mentioned it . . . or if you looked sideways at the gorgeous but brassy Japanese girl on his arm. An oversized purse hung from the girl's shapely bronze shoulder. The bulkier man looked slightly pissed, as if he'd not wanted to bring the girl, but had lost out.

The threesome turned down a side street and moved away from the lights. After five more turns to ensure they were not being followed, they entered a small restaurant. Kurimoto asked for a table, while discreetly making a certain hand gesture. The waiter led them into a small, deserted dining area—and kept a lookout while they moved onward through a hidden door behind the bar.

They came into a wide, low-ceilinged room, lit by recessed pot lights. More than a hundred men were interspersed among gambling tables. There were no other women.

"Who the hell is this?" A man with enormous shoulders and almost no hips demanded, standing in Kurimoto's way, his calloused finger directly in Sam's face.

"My 'cousin' Seiji from Osaka, Yakamen-san," said Kurimoto. "He was in town and naturally wanted to know anything there is to know about what's going on here."

The man, still blocking their way, looked over Sam. "Who do you answer to in Osaka?"

"Tetsuo Nogami, *fuku-honbucho* to Masaru Takumi," answered Sam truculently. "Listen, if people are dying indiscriminately in Tokyo, I'm not going to sit in a sake bar like a fucking tourist."

"You have a lot of fingers for somebody with such a big mouth."

"We don't screw up in Takumi's family," Sam said, and threw an insolent glance at the missing joint on the big man's hand.

The big man glared at him for a long moment. On an ordinary night Yakamen might have taken Sam aside and held him while he called Osaka . . . but this wasn't an ordinary night. The meeting had been hastily called, and he trusted Kurimoto . . . The big man stepped aside to admit them.

Jen might just as well have not been there. Until she passed the big man by, that is. He leered long and hard at her luscious silk-clad hips. Japanese girls didn't often have an ass like that.

The three newcomers made their way across the room, with Kurimoto greeting men along the way. Others entered the room through the restaurant behind them. Within five minutes the room was packed, stuffy, and hot. The two unknown attendees were lost in the crowd, forgotten.

At the front of the room, a middle-aged man stood, and the crowd grew quickly silent. This man was impeccably dressed, like a financier, and for the past ten yeas he had, in fact, been one. The relationship between the Yakuza and Japanese banks is a close one, as the Yakuza is the country's top corporate earner, toting up eight times the income of Toyota.

This was Masahisa Takenaka, "father" of the *Yamaguchi-gumi.*

"Gentlemen, we assemble tonight in the fact of a grave threat to our nation . . . but with the great respect of our nation's enemies. The men who detonated the Sarin bomb have contacted me."

A subdued murmur darted through the room. Sam and Kurimoto looked at each other. Jen had no idea what was said but could tell they were disturbed.

"I was unable to persuade these people to reveal their identity. The contact was oblique. But they offered proof that they were, indeed, the men responsible. They wanted me to know that they plan a second attack in two days. They will explode another bomb within the Ministry of Finance. They do not want us to suffer any harm from it."

"We can surely pull our men out before the bombing," said a fat man who wheezed with each breath. This was Takenaka's senior advisor, Nakanishi. "But I'm not sure we should allow another attack."

"I disagree," said Kishimoto, the headquarters chieftain, who looked like a wispy shadow in his dark, pinstriped suit. "The opportunities in the black market and protection will be enormous after such a blast. And since we're not responsible, there is no downside."

"There is the loss of men, women, and children," answered Nakanishi indignantly.

"It is the Yakuza's place to profit from the misfortunes of others."

"I agree," said Takenaka calmly. "These madmen will be caught in due time. They will not be connected with us. The opportunity presents itself."

"What if they kill members of the family by acci-

dent? Indiscriminate murder can't be controlled, no
matter their intentions," said Nakanishi. There was
no objection; it was his job to look for holes in his
"father's" schemes.

"Then," said Takenaka, "they will all die at our
hands. But the fact that they contacted me argues that
they do not fear that consequence."

He looked over the group. "Pass the word: no one
is to come within fifteen blocks of the Ministry of
Finance this Tuesday. Furthermore, a well-stocked
black market in chlorinated lime and magnesium
oxide, the agents of decontamination, will be sold for
profit from the aftermath. Yes?"

"Yes!" thundered the crowd, as one.

Takenaka sat down and the people began to dis-
perse; the assembly was over as suddenly as it had
begun. There was a great feeling of confidence and
relief among the Yakuza. But not among Kurimoto,
Sam, and Jen.

They exited into an alleyway behind the restaurant.
Men were leaving in every direction; they chose the
direction with the fewest people.

"What did they say—" began Jen, but Kurimoto
motioned fiercely for her to be quiet. She wondered
why, but as soon as they turned down another narrow
alley, they came face to face with Yakamen. Jennifer
darted a glance at Kurimoto. How had he known?

The big man laid a massive hand on Jen's arm.
"Perhaps you three would join me for some sake . . .
like a fucking tourist." He smiled. The smile was for
Jen alone; though it was meant to be charming, it was
extremely unsettling. Even though Jen didn't know
what he was saying, his smile made his intentions
much too obvious.

"Sorry to disappoint," Sam said, laying his own
hand over the big man's, "but now that I know what's
going on in Tokyo, we'll be getting the hell out of
here as soon as possible."

Yakamen ignored him. His eyes were locked on

Jen's face. "Have you seen the sights of Tokyo, my dear? There are places no Osakan should ever miss."

"We're leaving," said Sam more firmly, using his skill in the martial arts to pry the man's hand off Jen's arm.

"She'll have to tell me that herself."

Jen smiled and bowed her head. How long could she get by without speaking? She was a hell of an actress but you had to know your lines. She wanted no part of this. There should have been other people using this alley at this time of night, but for some reason, they were alone. No one wanted to stumble on Yakuza business.

"Which part of 'no' don't you understand, Yakamen?" Sam demanded, bravely getting in the big man's face and putting himself between him and Jen.

Kurimoto, too, pushed forward. "With respect, 'big brother,' you have no business with this woman."

Yakamen grabbed Kurimoto's hand and held the mutilated little finger high. "With respect," he said sneeringly, "you don't tell me what to do."

Sam knew you didn't have to be a chess grandmaster in order to see fives moves ahead in this conversation. He saw where this was bound to go. He abruptly shoved Kurimoto aside. "Stay out of this!" he snapped at the undercover man. "You're not involved. Go far away and be seen while I settle with this *pig*!"

The big man's eyes gleamed. His hand darted toward his hip and came back with a .40-caliber Glock automatic. But in the same instant Sam had plunged his hands into Jennifer's big purse and come up with a Tec-9 assault rifle. "I'll show you a part of Tokyo you haven't seen," he told the big man. "The part you see from six feet under. Now get the fuck away from my woman!"

In response, a sudden fusillade of shots exploded from a balcony one flight above the alley. If Sam hadn't been so close to Yakamen he'd have been a

sitting duck, but as it was, the shooter blasted the
street to his right, hoping to startle him into moving
left and becoming more visible. But it didn't happen.

Sam kneed Yakamen in the groin and crouched as
the big man sagged. Simultaneously, he swung his Tec-
9 around and blasted back at the balcony. Beside him,
Jen was flat against the alley wall, pulling her own
Glock from the bag. Kurimoto was still pawing at his
jacket, trying to get at his own weapon.

"Get out of here now!" snapped Sam. "You've got
a job to do!"

Kurimoto hesitated.

"Which part of 'go' don't you understand?!"

Kurimoto ran, as Sam and Jen threw covering fire.

Yakamen was on his knees, shaking off the effects
of the groin punch. He reached out and grabbed Sam's
leg, then threw him like a doll into the center of the
alleyway. Sam had no time to react: suddenly he was
flat on his back, his rifle skidding away from him on
the pavement. The pinging shots from above shifted
toward him. But Jennifer leapt into the alley beside
him and fired off her entire clip at the room. There
was a choking cry, then the sound of metal falling to
the floor. A man tumbled headfirst over the room's
balcony and landed on the pavement with a sound
like a ripe melon.

A massive fist hit Jen behind the left ear and sent
her sprawling. Yakamen body-slammed Sam and
wrapped his hands around Sam's skinny throat. He
was wasting no time on this twerp: one twist meant
one less punk from Osaka. But before he could make
his move Sam slammed his right arm against the
street. With the slightest of sounds, a hunting knife
popped out from a hidden holster directly into Sam's
right hand. He drove the blade upward into Yakamen's stomach and ripped toward the sternum. Sam's
own stomach lurched as he felt warm blood and guts
spill onto his suit. But Yakamen didn't seem to notice.
He grinned and tensed his massive shoulders for the

killing twist. Sam fought to hold his neck straight, but the pressure was too great.

And then there was no pressure at all.

Yakamen looked down at himself, confused, and then vomited blood. His massive hands dropped away from Sam's neck and then the big man slumped forward on the knife.

Sam leveraged the dead man off his stomach, helped by Jennifer. Now that the moment was past, his legs were a tad rubbery as she helped him stand. "Damn, Sam!" she said. "You da man!" She hugged him with uninhibited enthusiasm. For this moment, Sam was content to hug her back, glad to have kept down his dinner at the sight of all the gore.

Then he heard Kurimoto's voice from far away, yelling, "It came from this direction! Hurry!"

"He's bringing more Yakuza," Sam said. "He's maintaining his cover. But he doesn't want to catch us any more than we want to be caught."

Jennifer nodded. She let Sam go and ran her eyes over the alley, to see if they had left anything that would reveal they'd been there. She saw nothing, and neither did Sam. Gathering the Tec-9, the two of them raced away into the Tokyo night.

Chapter 8

The seven members of TALON Force Eagle Team
formed a tight circle in the secluded officers' quarters
assigned to them for the duration of their stay at Yokota. Sam gave them an almost word-for-word run-
down on what he'd heard at the meeting. Neither he
nor Jennifer told them what he'd done afterward, because it wasn't relevant to their immediate problem.

The Yakuza hadn't set off the Sarin bombs.

They were not the ones who had sent a message to
the NSA threatening the American embassy.

"So," said Travis, "we don't know our enemy, after
all."

"If it's even *our* enemy," said Stan. "If American
interests aren't at stake, TALON has no business
here."

"But *somebody* threatened the embassy," objected
Sarah. "Maybe they lied about who they were, but the
threat remains."

"Maybe," said Stan. "And maybe the whole thing's
some sick freak's idea of a joke."

"Are you prepared to walk away, then, Stan?"
asked Hunter.

"I'm just saying, we don't know why we're here
now."

"So we have to find out," said Travis. "And evidently, the real guys are going to be at the Ministry of Finance in thirty-six hours. That's our best chance."

"It could be a diversion from an embassy attack at the same time," suggested Jen.

"Yes, indeed," said Travis. "But embassy security belongs to the Marines. We'll make sure they're on extra-high alert and station Sam and Jen there, since they've already had some action." He nodded at the blood on their clothes; he didn't have to be told they'd been busy. "But the most credible threat is the one conveyed to the Yakuza, because there's no good reason for it to be a lie. And nobody fucks with the Yakuza if they don't have to. So the rest of us will be at the Ministry." He turned to Sam. "Meanwhile, I want *you* to get your hard disk in gear and find out who sent that message to the NSA. Nobody fucks with the U-S-of-A, either."

"It'll be a pleasure, Trav," Sam answered.

Chapter 9

Tuesday morning dawned with the bright, eye-searing haze that congested streets seem to spawn. Car exhausts and cooking fumes seem as reluctant to leave the city as your average resident. Small wonder Japan boasts more sunglasses per person than any other place on earth, including the Mideastern desert kingdoms.

The five *gaijin* who haunted the Ministry of Finance in business attire also wore glasses, but these special shades allowed them to look anywhere and everywhere without seeming to. They were able to stay in voice contact through the Micro-Biochip Transmitter/Receivers implanted along their jaws.

The implant was a voice transmitter that allowed TALON Force troopers to talk to each other without the need for an external microphone. It could transmit and receive on its own, using line-of-sight transmissions within a range of one thousand meters. At other times, when the troopers wore their Battle Ensembles, they could talk directly to Joint Task Force Headquarters by satellite transmission.

Everyone who entered the Ministry building was watched through one or more of the special glasses. The most potent part of this procedure was the watching, as every member of TALON Force had spent the past two days learning the faces and characteristics of the major players in the non-Yakuza underworld.

Anyone who drew more than passing attention warranted an almost-insignificant hand signal from the observing member to a member of Kurimoto's task force. That Japanese agent stepped forward and invited the suspect to step aside for a brief chat. In so doing, the suspect stepped in front of a pair of hidden cameras, which snapped photographs in full-face and profile, then beamed it off to the computers of the National Identification Section. Within six minutes a full report on the suspect was in Kurimoto's hands at his command center on the mezzanine.

From the moment the building opened until 2:47 P.M., 432 people entered. Forty-six were checked and cleared. Then came number forty-seven.

Outwardly, he was like most everyone else who had entered the building that day: a trim man gone somewhat to seed through soft middle-aged living, but cocooned in a thousand-dollar suit that almost succeeded in hiding his paunch. He carried an alligator briefcase, which rolled through an X-ray without showing anything out of the ordinary as he traded pleasant banter with the guard. However, Travis, who was stationed nearby, kept his shaded eyes locked on the man's eyes and saw them flick skyward when he had to sign in. It was an old trick Travis had learned through countless interrogations with Delta Force: if the eyes glanced up and to the left, one was searching his memory; if they went up and to the right, one was brewing bullshit. These were definitely bullshit eyes.

Travis flicked his forefinger once, like a catcher signaling a fastball. The task force member drifted into the stranger's path.

"Excuse me, sir. A moment of your time, please."

The man drew himself up. "I'm late for an appointment. Some other time."

The Japanese agent smiled, all teeth. "It will only take a moment. This way, please." He wrapped his fingers around the man's elbow and gave the slightest press. There was nothing a legitimate businessman could have complained about afterward, but anyone would immediately realize that increased pressure would certainly result in pain, impacting the nerves bundled there. It generated a subliminal, almost instinctive agreement to come along.

The two men stepped into an alcove off the main hall. Three vases of fresh-cut flowers bracketed them, so that no matter which way the man turned he'd face one and be side-on to another.

"It's just routine, sir," said the task force member. "The Sarin attacks, you understand. If I could just have your home address or hotel suite . . ."

Meanwhile, a woman entered. She, too, was well-dressed and calm, but the purse that hung off her right shoulder seemed to hang abnormally low. Travis watched closely as she removed the purse for the X-ray machine—and noticed that her shoulder remained low. He was not surprised when the machine showed nothing to give the attendant alarm. Nevertheless, Travis's finger flicked again. If the purse weren't weighing her down, then she was either deformed . . . or she had spent a lot of time with something that was very heavy slung over that shoulder. Something like a rifle. He had seen it time and again in revolutionary or military cultures.

A second Japanese agent invited her to a second alcove for a brief chat, even as the first agent was passing the first suspect on through. Soon she, too, was released with the agent's polite thanks. If either one of them was dirty, the forces of order would know within less than ten minutes. That was not enough time for anyone to reach any vital center of the Ministry and get out again.

So far we've been wrong forty-six times, thought Travis as his eyes locked on the next man coming in. It didn't bother him in the slightest. He was prepared to be wrong 146 more times—1,046. He would stand at his post all day long, never restless, never slouched, and do what he had to do to protect this city.

"TALON."

The Micro-Biochip implant spoke for the first time in two hours. He responded in a low murmur, the bones in his head carrying the sound to the mike but not to anyone more than two feet away.

"What's up, Saval?" Other voices were responding all along the line.

"The computers just went down. It could just be an overload. I'll know more in a minute. But you'll have to deal with suspicious strangers on your own 'til further notice."

Travis's eyes still hadn't left the entryway, but now he was thinking. "TALON—I just had two suspects over here. Anybody else?"

"Nothing on this side."

"Quiet for the past ten."

All around the horn came more negatives.

"Stan—Jack—meet me at the elevator." Travis motioned to Kurimoto, already moving out. The Japanese major pointed at another agent. "You're in charge." He ran to catch up to Travis.

Stan and Jack were running, too, as they all converged at the block of twelve elevators. People were entering and leaving them, but Travis stepped in front of one whose doors had opened, blocking the people waiting for it.

"Get them out, Kurimoto-san!"

The Japanese barked polite but short orders, and the men and women inside the elevator hurried out. He bowed his thanks to the waiting group as he and the three TALON Force members got onto the car.

"Where was the last man questioned going?" Travis asked Kurimoto.

"Patent office, fourteenth floor."

"He's probably anyplace but there, but we'll check it out first." Travis punched the button and they shot upward. He explained on the way. "Two suspicious characters back to back, and then we can't run a check? I'm not buying it."

"What about the second man?" asked Jack.

"It was a woman. I didn't get where she was going. My fault."

Travis spoke using the benefit of his implant. "Sarah, go to my post and ask the agent there where the woman he checked said she was going. Grab Hunter and find her."

"On my way."

The doors opened on the fourteenth floor. Kurimoto leapt out and engaged in rapid conversation with the receptionist, then turned back. "She hasn't seen either one of them."

"Tell her to keep her eyes open."

"I did."

"Then get back in."

Travis punched the button for twenty-two and sent them rocketing toward the top floor. He then said, "Jack, get off here and work your way down to sixteen. We'll take fifteen to the ground floor in five-floor sections. Kurimoto, start telling us what these people look like."

Kurimoto gave a precise description of the suspects before Jack got off and the elevator headed back down. He flashed a card provided by Kurimoto at the receptionist but didn't wait to see if she responded. He just burst through the double doors.

Inside, security men moved to block his way. This was the office of the minister of finance. They didn't need words to make themselves understood. Jack didn't either; the card would make his point. But not knowing Japanese, he might not be able to ask them if they'd seen his pigeons.

"Have you seen a man or a woman enter here in the last three minutes? *Est-ce que un homme ou une femme est arrivé dans trois minutes? ¿Ha llegado un hombre o una mujer entre tres minutos?*" The Ministry of Finance dealt with fiscal organizations across the globe. Someone had to speak a foreign language.

"Je parle français," said the receptionist, a petite woman—was there any other kind in Japan?—with pretty, intelligent eyes. She had followed Jack into the office.

"Venez, ma belle," said Jack, taking her arm gently but firmly and heading deeper into the ministry. *"Vite!"*

He explained to her who he was working for. She hadn't seen them. But he kept her moving along with him as they took the emergency stairs down to twenty-one, where she put the question in Japanese to the workers there. They shook their heads, so Jack led her down to twenty.

They had no luck until they reached the seventeenth floor.

"The man left just thirty seconds ago," said an office worker in a ragged waistcoat, pointing toward the front of the office suite. Jack squeezed his companion's arm, surprisingly gently considering his strength and excitement. *"Merci, ma petite,"* he rapped out, and ran in the direction of Waistcoat's finger.

"Pas de problème," she whispered to his back.

Jack burst through the intervening doors in time to see his quarry punch the button for the elevator. His entrance caused the man to spin and see him as well—then the guy bolted for the front fire stairs. Jack was close behind him, and as he clattered down the stairs he radioed the others: "Male suspect heading for sixteen, on the front stairs!"

"I'm on thirteen," answered Stan. "We'll sandwich the son of a bitch!"

If the fleeing man had tried to get off at fifteen Jack was prepared to beat him a little harder than he already had planned, but Mr. Speedo ran past the exit door and kept descending. Intent on his pursuer, the man wasn't ready at all for the door on the thirteenth floor to be flung open right in his face. Which is why

it was so amazing that he somehow managed to dodge
the door with lightning agility and leap past Stan Powczuk into the hallway without breaking stride. Jack
slipped Stan trying to get past him and lost a precious
second. The two of them pounded after their quarry,
who showed no signs of tiring.

Secretaries screamed and patent papers flew as the
man scrambled away down the center aisle. Stan had
his gun out but couldn't chance a shot in the melee.
The man headed straight for the back stairs and disappeared again.

Stan and Jack, piling into the stairwell, heard foot-
steps clattering above their heads. "This guy is pissing
me off!" snapped Jack.

"Not in shape, gyrene?" asked Stan, bolting upward.

Jack matched him stride for stride. "After we get
done, I'll kick your ass and then you can tell me."

Up they went, past fifteen and sixteen. The guy was
a full flight ahead of them so neither man could get
off a shot, but gradually Jack and Stan closed the gap.
By the eighteenth floor, Jack put a round just behind
the guy's flying heels, and on nineteen, the quarry fled
through the door.

Four seconds later, Stan and Jack followed him, but
came to a quick halt. The floor was unoccupied, and
in all that emptiness there was no sound of running
feet. As one, they dived for cover as a precaution,
Stan to the left and Jack right.

No one shot at them but their guy had to be in the
room. Jack snapped his hand in front of his mouth in
a wiping motion. Stan took a breath and held it. He
could do it for three minutes, even after exerting himself as he'd done just now. Jack listened.

His boyhood in the bayou paid off. Ears trained to
hear gators swimming in the swamps heard soft
breathing three aisles ahead. It was shallow breathing,
controlled, but Jack couldn't miss it. He wiped off his
earlier motion and Stan let his air out silently. Jack

held up three fingers and motioned toward Stan's side of the aisle ahead.

Stan nodded and slid into a prone position. Peering under the desks he could see a large wastebasket three rows ahead . . . and a shoe sticking out behind it. Stan began a crawl, flat on his belly, underneath the desks. Across the aisle Jack was doing the same thing.

Now Stan could hear the breathing clearly. If the guy jumped up and ran now, the TALON Force guys would lose any advantage they had before they could get out from under the desks.

Stan was now only one desk away. He would still have to cross the space between this one and the one the guy was using as a shield. He paused long enough to be sure the other guy's breathing wasn't speeding up prior to a jump, then wiggled his way forward.

As he got within grabbing distance of the guy's foot, Jack slammed his fist into another wastebasket across the aisle. It went flying with a shocking crash, causing the guy to shift his feet in order to flee. It also brought his shoe that much closer to Stan's position. Stan swept it out from under him, and the guy went down hard in the aisle. By the time he got his wits about him Jack had a gun planted against his temple.

Stan, coming up behind, laid his own gun on the desk and did a thorough two-handed search. It came up empty.

"Kurimoto, Travis—Jack and I have our male suspect on nineteen. How do you say, 'Where's the bomb?' " Stan asked over his implant.

Kurimoto told him, and Stan parroted the sounds at the prone man. The man grunted something in return that needed no translation.

"Kurimoto, how do you say, 'Where's the bomb, you son of a bitch?' " Then without waiting for an answer, he said, "Ah, the hell with it," and kicked the guy where it would get his attention.

By the time Travis and Kurimoto arrived, the prisoner was talking freely, but they needed Kurimoto to tell them what he said. "It boils down to the fact that he doesn't have the bomb but he'll be damn glad when it goes off and takes you two out."

"A decoy?" asked Stan.

"We can check," said Travis, kneeling down with a chemical sniffer. He studied the readouts and announced, "He's been around Sarin but there's not enough for him to be the carrier."

"A decoy!" bitched Jack. "Then it's got to be the woman."

"Sarah," said Travis to his throat mike, "we need the woman."

"She got out of the building, Travis. Security wasn't looking at people leaving. Hunter and I are on the streets searching."

"We'll be right down." Travis yanked the prisoner to his feet by his collar and shoved him toward the front of the offices. They went through the standard double doors and pressed the elevator button.

"What's it mean to you, to kill hundreds or thousands of innocent people?" Kurimoto asked him in Japanese.

"In the twenty-first century nobody's innocent," the guy answered with a sneer. "Not me, not you, not them."

The elevator farthest down the bank arrived. The other eleven, Stan noticed, hadn't moved, probably incapacitated by Sarah to narrow the way out. They piled into the car and Travis hit the lobby button. They rocketed downward.

No one had anything else to say . . . until Jack suddenly spoke. "This guy's breathing's speeded up."

Everyone looked at the prisoner, who stared back with a strange, determined light in his eyes. Almost without thinking, Stan stabbed the STOP button. The elevator came to a shuddering halt, halfway between floors three and two.

Stan turned to the doors and slowly wrenched them apart. Jack stepped forward and shoved his gun between them as they tried to automatically close. Stan dropped again to a prone position and leaned over the car's floor, his eyes peering down the shaft.

The prisoner lunged forward to kick him into the abyss, but Travis had been watching him closely and slammed him back against the car's far wall.

Stan's voice came echoing from what seemed a long way away. "Guess what—the bomb's on the bottom of the car. We were supposed to set it off ourselves when we touched the bottom floor." He twisted back up and around, a crooked smile on his face. "I like it. I like it a lot."

Chapter 10

There was nothing likeable about the island of Kamasho, sixty-seven storm-swept miles off the bleak
coast of Hokkaido. Until 1945 it had been an outpost
in the Japanese Home Guard, keeping a bleary eye
out for Americans sailing out of the Pacific's blue.
They never saw any, and after the surrender it was
gratefully abandoned by all but lost fishermen. But in
the early '60s, these random visitors found themselves
turned back by smart-looking cruisers. If they'd persisted and somehow found their way onto the rocky
beaches, they'd have uncovered nothing more than the
weather-beaten shacks and bunkers left from the war.
Of course, if they'd *really* persisted and entered the
shacks, they'd have found brand-new metal stairways
leading downward—and that would have been the last
thing they'd ever have uncovered.

Because down those metal stairways was the new
interrogation center for Japanese Intelligence. And as
the interrogators liked to say after the *Alien* movie
came out in the '80s, "On Kamasho, no one can hear
you scream."

TALON Force was invited down these very stairs
by Kurimoto and they took a look around, but interrogation wasn't all that interesting to them, for the most
part. There are certain time-tested techniques that

they knew as well as anyone and were prepared to use themselves as it became necessary on a mission, but the Japanese weren't showing them anything new. So after the first morning everyone but Jack and Sarah went back to Yokota Air Force Base and waited for the results.

Jack stuck around because he had a natural appreciation for the application of psychological pressure and pain. And, as he cheerfully quoted Sarah from *The Art of War*: "Advance knowledge cannot be gained from ghosts and spirits, inferred from phenomena, or projected from the measures of Heaven, but must be gained from men for it is the knowledge of the enemy's true situation."

Sarah stuck around as well, to learn what she could about the Sarin. Kurimoto's question before TALON Force entered the Ministry of Finance's elevator had been recounted to her, and it echoed at the edges of her mind: "What's it mean to you, to kill hundreds or thousands of innocent people?"

There were times when she wanted to look away from the interrogation, but she steeled her eyes. Overcoming any weakness within her for the sake of TALON was a constant theme with her, but it was more than that.

Hundreds or thousands of innocent people.

She knew what those people looked like when they died.

Innocent people.

Captain Sarah Greene watched it all.

Chapter 11

Lieutenant Sarah Greene moved through the make-shift wards at St. Luke's International Hospital, check-ing on 460 of her patients. She hadn't slept since the transport from Germany had set down at Yokota AFB thirty-seven hours ago, and she was finding it harder and harder to move. But the idea of going to sleep appalled her. Every minute she slept was a minute in which one of her patients could slip into the big sleep. Sure, there were other doctors, incredibly trained doc-tors, from all over the world. It was the nature of the world community to help with disasters such as this one, and she wasn't anywhere near arrogant enough to think that she was indispensable to these patients. But they were *her* patients. Men, women, and so many children, that she'd committed herself to keeping alive if there was any way in hell, and she wasn't going to go to sleep until each and every one was out of danger . . . or beyond help.

"Sarah?"

"Yes, Olaf?" It was a Norwegian doctor who'd ar-rived sometime after she had. She'd never spoken five words to him, but they'd run into each other probably two dozen times over the past day and a half.

"You need sleep, Sarah."

"Fuck you, Olaf."

She didn't say it with animosity, or with irony, or with anything at all. She had no energy for emotions like that. But he understood, and smiled—he could still smile, so he *must* have started later than she did, or awakened from a recent nap. He patted her shoulder and moved on toward his ward.

She pulled one of her clip-on earrings from a pocket and stuck it on her ear—then pressed it against the lobe, hard. The sudden pain made her a little sharper. She walked back through the ward to the beginning, then turned and started working her way through her patients again.

Mrs. Hanai wasn't there any more. Nor was Mr. Makino. And the little Takeoka boy. Every time she passed this way there were fewer. But at least the empty cots weren't being refilled with new victims. Those who were going to succumb to the nerve agent had done so.

Three beds down, Mr. Akagaki began to spasm, choking on the mucus that oozed from his throat. A Japanese nurse raced toward him, but Sarah got there first. She grabbed the curved plastic tube and inserted it, forcefully yet gently, down the old man's windpipe, keeping the passage open. The nurse drew a quantity of atropine from a vial, pushed any air bubbles out, and injected Akagaki. He grew quieter, but Sarah didn't like his look. He had been greatly weakened. As she watched, his face grew darker, bluer, even though the airway was now open.

"Another 10 cc!" Sarah said, but before the nurse could administer it, Akagaki stopped breathing. Sarah began to administer CPR—chest only. No one could risk giving mouth-to-mouth to a man struck down by a nerve agent. Under her hands, Sarah could feel the weak cardiac rhythm.

"God damn you!" she gritted. "You know what I'm saying? You bet you do! Get your act together, Akagaki! Get that heart going! You hear me?"

A phrase from her dim Jewish upbringing resounded in her ears as she rocked rhythmically on his chest. *"L'chaim! L'chaim! L'chaim!"* To life! To life! To life!

"Code blue!" she yelled at the nurse, only to find that the nurse already had the heart stimulator there. Sarah ripped open the old man's shirt and let the nurse place the two defibrillator panels. "Clear!" The panels surged with electricity and the old man surged in his bed . . . but his heart did not restart. "Clear! Give him a second dose!"

"He's gone, Sarah."

"Clear!"

"He's gone, Sarah."

"Clear, dammit!"

"He's—"

"Okay, okay . . . I hear you." She moved away from the bed and let out a deep sigh. It was Olaf. He put an arm around her—awkwardly, since at 5'4" she was a foot and a half shorter than he was.

"You need sleep, Sarah."

"I didn't screw up."

"I didn't say you did. You haven't screwed up in thirty-seven hours, according to the staff here. But you need sleep."

"Not yet."

"Go get some rest, Sarah. We'll cope. I'll need you to spell me when I fade out."

"Fuck you, Olaf."

"I'll need you to do that, too."

It took her a second to realize what he'd said. Then abruptly, she burst out in a giggle.

"Neither one of us has the energy."

"Speak for yourself, woman. Now go."

She bit her lip, but nodded. "Okay. Okay. I have something to do, anyway."

She found Brigadier General Jack Krauss at the temporary command center set up outside the contaminated area. He looked tired, too. Everybody did.

"Lieutenant Greene? You look like hell."

"Can't. I just got propositioned."

He smiled, but said, "I don't have much time, Lieutenant. What can I do for you?"

"That project you're working on. The one—"

"Yes," Krauss said, looking quickly around. He moved her away from the personnel bustling around the center to a quieter corner. "I remember."

"You wanted somebody who would kill if necessary."

"Among other things."

"Well, when we talked before, I had always seen medicine as a way to save people—even the enemy, if it came to that. But now . . . now I see that one way to save people is to rid the world of monsters like the people who did this. Some people just don't deserve to live."

"I'm glad you understand that, Lieutenant." A rueful smile played across his craggy face. "But I've made my recommendation, and we've moved on. I'm sorry— you're too late."

Chapter 12

It took twenty-eight hours for the prisoner to crack. Sarah finally went to sleep, completely worn out from watching, and when she woke up there was Jack happily telling her they had what they needed.

The two TALON Force members, along with Kurimoto, took a Japanese Army helicopter back down to Yokota, where they broke up the pick-up basketball game Travis, Stan, and Jen were playing with the airmen in their hangar. Sam was keeping score and Hunter was busy checking the specs of an F-117 Nighthawk with its pilot. After Hunter came running and the airmen were sent packing—just as they were about to win!—TALON Force and its liaison conferred, their lowered voices echoing from the hangar's curved metal walls.

Kurimoto said, "The perpetrator's name is Tsoy Ah Lim. He works for the Ch'u Triad, whom we know to be a major criminal enterprise in Hong Kong. The Triad was an outlaw among outlaws before the mainland takeover; they'd do the big work, and the work others had risen above. Evidently if the money was right, the Ch'u Triad had no scruples at all. There's always a place for people like that in a system built on hard cash, but after the takeover, the authorities went after the Triad with a vengeance. Like all the

Triads who made their money on the black market engendered by the British colony on the one hand and the Chinese mainland on the other, the Ch'u Triad was said to have lost much of its influence after the 1997 reunification. However, unlike other Triads that left the colony and moved to America and Canada, this Triad has remained. We frankly have not maintained the *intensity* of our information on the Chinese Triad situation since ninety-seven, as it appeared the Chinese government was effectively hamstringing it."

"I should add," said Sarah, "that while we were flying back I was in contact with the C.I.A. in Washington." What she meant but didn't say in front of Kurimoto was that she'd been in contact with Brigadier General Jack Krauss, TALON Force's commander, who worked under Chairman of the Joint Chiefs of Staff General George H. Gates. It was General Krauss's staff that had done the legwork in Washington. "The C.I.A., too, has kept an eye on the Hong Kong gangs, but mostly with an eye toward any movement toward America. But apparently, American interests have little trouble with the Ch'u Triad if they maintain a cordial business relationship with a man called Norman Pin Wong. Speculation is common that Pin Wong runs the Triad, and speculation is rarely wrong in these matters. But nothing has ever been proved, or even close to proved."

"That is so," said Kurimoto. "In effect, Norman Pin Wong occupies a space similar to that of the Triads before the reunification. He does business internationally through Hong Kong, and internally with Beijing. Therefore, he is a useful middleman for both sides. And he is highly successful. If he runs the Ch'u Triad, his daring—as you Americans say, 'chutzpah'—is colossal. And I say 'if' because we have never obtained any hard evidence against him, either."

"So then," said Travis, "our friend in the island basement didn't mention his name."

"Exactly. We asked, very politely, but he is far too

removed from the heights of the Triad to know its leader by name."

"What about the American embassy, or the Yakuza?"

"He knows nothing about either. Personally, I am convinced that the Triad had nothing to do with that threat."

"And he doesn't know who does?"

"No."

"I don't like it," said Travis. "We're getting closer to the truth but we're not getting all of it. There's a joker in the deck somewhere."

"Again, Lim is just one of the Triad's soldiers. Men like him never know the grand plan. He and his female accomplice—his wife, it turns out—were sent here to detonate the bombs. Her name is Gwyneth."

"Gwyneth?"

"She's British."

"Ah."

"They received both bombs, along with instructions, from their lieutenant, whose name is Gee Po, at a deserted spot on the coast last week. He hasn't seen Gee Po since. He gave us the address he and Gwyneth had occupied, but of course she's long gone. However, we also managed to learn the location of the Ch'u Triad's base in China. It is hidden inside a cave that, quote 'looks like a falcon, six miles inland, where the Pearl River twists like a snake.' Our cartographers are using satellite imagery to determine the exact location as we speak."

"*That's* more like it," said Stan. "Did he tell you what size force we can expect to meet there?"

"He believes there are at least thirty men. It is their safe haven during the upheavals in Hong Kong and is run by the highest-ranking Triad member he knows, a Mr. Wu. Our prisoner is convinced that Mr. Wu knows the overall Triad plan."

Chapter 13

TALON Force's C-117 Globemaster took off from Yokota Air Force Base at dusk that night, and headed southwest for Singapore.

As the transport flew toward Taiwan, it climbed steadily, so that when it passed between the island and Hong Kong on the mainland, a little farther south, it was at 38,000 feet. The pilot, a young man from South Bend, Indiana, was on the horn with PRC air traffic controllers, telling them how much he liked flying along their coastline, because it recalled the stories older pilots had told him about the days when America and China were allies against the Japanese, and Pappy Chenault and the Flying Tigers had plied their trade above the South China Sea. He was totally sincere; he loved that stuff. But beyond that, the direction the Chinese would take in the twenty-first century was still up in the air. Their Communist heritage could lead them to become the major villain of the new century, or their capitalist connections could lead them to become a key player in the global community. The pilot much preferred the peaceful scenario and liked to talk with the Chinese as friends, in hopes that he might be one of the many little things that would convince the Chinese that joining the free world was the best way to go. A journey of a thousand miles, of course, begins with a single step.

Back in the passenger compartment, Sam was huddled over his laptop, taking the opportunity to work on the message that had been sent to the NSA claiming Yakuza responsibility for the Sarin bombs. General Krauss had had an exact copy of the original downloaded to TALON Force's electronics whiz kid, and Sam was in seventh heaven.

"Getting anywhere?" asked Travis, after watching him punch keys in a frenzy.

"The message is 'postmarked' from Bern, Switzerland," said Sam, "but that's just a blind. The site's a remailer. Messages come in and are resent so that they—theoretically—can't be traced."

"But you can defeat the theory."

"Piece o' cake. I burrow down through the internal addresses and reconfigure—"

"Spare me the details," said Travis. "That's your world, not mine. But you've got the sender?"

"Oh no. The Bern site leads back to Liberia, and I'm sure there'll be several more connections before that one. But I'll get it eventually."

"Well, you sure won't get it right now, because we're about to move out."

"Damn! A guy can't have any fun."

The pilot and his Chinese friends were chortling over tales of the Burma runs when the red light on his console showed the pilot that the side door was open. He didn't miss a beat as he made the slight corrections for a plane now carrying seven fewer passengers.

TALON Force dropped toward the Chinese coast using their HALO (High Altitude, Low Opening) chutes. The nominal use for HALO was to let them jump out of a plane at an altitude where no one expected a jump, free falling until the very last second, when their chutes' opening was least likely to be seen. The C-117 Globemaster could only "lumber" so far off course because the friendly Chinese air traffic controllers would order a correction. The TALON team could land in the water if they had to, but it would add several more steps to their infiltration, so they preferred to spread their arms and legs, air-surfing their way as far toward land as possible.

Traveling well over two hundred miles an hour, the team was right at the height of the low, rolling coastal hills when their chutes opened. The shock was as extreme as the highly trained human body could stand. Any more and their eyeballs would spew out of their heads as they broke their necks, any less and they'd drive their feet into their eyeballs when they smacked the ground. Each member of the Force had trained long hours to find their personal limit, and each of their chutes was calibrated exactly for their requirements.

They all hit the earth and rolled with the impact— and were on their feet instantly to pull the chute's lines and quickly collapse the canopy. Inside one minute, all seven were standing with their nylon in a pile beside them. They stripped the harnesses and rolled the chutes into highly compressed balls, then buried the balls in the hard, dry Chinese earth.

They were ready for the Ch'u Triad.

Chapter 14

The hour before dawn found them in a grove of trees, looking across a wide field of native grasses at the caves. There was no mistaking the place; the late moon threw low shadows but the "beak" of the falcon, made by a sharp overhanging crevice, was clearly visible. Bright ripples in the Pearl River revealed its meandering flow, making four tight snakelike turns to the north and south.

Ordinary commandos would be stymied by the field. There was no cover at all for over one hundred yards as you approached the cavern. A good infiltrator would have had to come in from above, down the cliff face. The field was open because it was deliberately kept that way. There was nothing obvious, but trained eyes could see that the trees came to too abrupt a halt here. There should have been smaller trees, seedlings—but there were no trees at all. There should have been occasional rocks dotting the field—there had certainly been rough country leading to this point—but likewise, there were none. Clearly, the Ch'u Triad had prepared their "front yard" to afford no cover to an approaching enemy, and it was reasonable to assume they'd taken similar precautions with the rocks above them. All that was left, for ordinary commandos, was a frontal assault—World War I tactics.

Unfortunately for the Ch'u Triad, warfare was a century further along. TALON Force had their Battle Ensembles.

The Battle Ensemble consists of a "brilliant suit" that provides full body armor protection; immediate and automatic medical trauma aid; a body heat or body cooling capability; voice, digital, and holographic communications; thermal ranging, laser designating, and high-powered optical sensing; and a "brilliant camouflage" capability. The suit has a normal power capacity of seventy-two hours without recharging—although the Low Observable Suite could only run continuously for six hours before draining the Battle Ensemble's charge.

Micro-sensors woven into the rough, bulletproof fabric of the ensemble automatically copy the exact shade, color, and luminosity of the background. In essence, the wearer becomes the background, blending in with the surroundings like a chameleon. The only thing seen by the naked eye is a slight shimmer.

The ensemble's Battle Sensor Helmet is made of light but extremely tough micro-fibers that act as ballistic protection. It is also a communications suite and computer network station, using the Micro-Biochip Transmitter/Receiver embedded under the trooper's skin.

Hidden by the deep moonshadows of the trees, the TALON teammates donned their ensembles and double-checked the equipment to make certain it hadn't suffered any damage from the HALO insertion.

"If I had to guess, I'd say their shift will be over at dawn," said Travis. "They'll be tired, looking forward to hitting the sack. Let's take them now."

As the moon slid below the western hills, TALON Force Eagle Team moved out. The light was uncertain—soft light was provided from the west by the moon and from the east by the coming sun. It was the perfect time to incorporate the Battle Ensembles' unique capabilities.

Seven across, but staggered in threes, the Force walked boldly across the field. Inside the cave, the sentries were alert. They were not expecting trouble, because all their operations were well away from China, but they knew the size of the stakes they were playing for and played accordingly. Even at the end of the dog watch they were not drowsy. They scanned the approach to their lair with intense vigilance. But they saw nothing they could comprehend as danger. A human-sized shimmer in the air was practically invisible in the changing light of dawn. A series of bent grass tracks was absorbed by the changing wind blowing over the field.

In other situations, the Triad was used to employing electronic sensors, but here at their headquarters they deemed it better to avoid those. A sensor could be stumbled across, sowing suspicion where there had been one. And so, sentries stared at the grass and waited for their shift to end at dawn.

It ended just a bit before that.

Suddenly seven people, evidently coordinated by unheard communication, burst into appearance right in front of them. The sentries opened their mouths to shout a warning, or jerked their AK-47s into position to fire, or turned to run for help—but none of it did them any good. Every Chinese in the cave mouth died before they were totally certain of what they were seeing.

"We want to keep as much reserve power for the ensemble batteries as we can," said Travis through the Battle Sensor Helmet Communications System. "As long as we can operate with the suits off, that's the way to go."

"Let's get out of this area, Travis," said Stan. "We don't have much time."

"We never have much time," answered Travis, as they started off into the cavern.

It soon became apparent why this cave had been chosen as the Triad's secret headquarters, and why it had served them so well. Once inside the man-sized opening, it expanded rapidly back into the rock. Within a few feet the roof was at least fifty feet above their heads. Their footfalls echoed from the stone walls, but so far they were the only ones around.

An elevator was carved out of the stone wall directly ahead.

"Left from mining days," said Sam.

"Look at it, though," said Jack. "That's up-to-date equipment."

Sam rolled his eyes. "Of course these guys refitted the elevator, but the shaft itself is obviously old. Look at the pick-axe marks."

Travis pushed the button beside the tight-fitting steel door. They heard the hum of a motor kick in.

"Pretty sharp," said Hunter. "An existing mine, abandoned or maybe not. The Triad buys it legally, claiming to be searching for gold or copper or whatever they dug out here—no need to try and hide."

"No *way* to try and hide in the most populous country on earth," said Jennifer. "Even if it weren't also a massive bureaucracy."

" 'Hello, Comrade Inspector. Let me show you our meager haul of nuggets. All of our records are in order,' " quipped Hunter. "While they hide the other stuff that goes on here."

"You're assuming that there are places to hide underground?" asked Travis.

"Aren't you?"

The hum stopped and the doors slid wide. It was a service elevator, built to handle mining equipment; it easily handled seven passengers. They piled inside and Travis pushed the button for the bottom floor, one level below. With a jerk and a hum they started down.

"How far do you think it goes?" asked Jen.

"It could be anything from ten to a hundred feet," answered Sam.

"Use your oxygen!" snapped Travis. He pointed toward a small opening high in the corner of the car.

The TALON Force members switched from breathing the outside air to internal oxygen with a flick of their eyes.

Within the Battle Sensor Helmet is the Battle Sensor Device. The BSD folds down over the left eye like a monocle and generates a laser pathway that paints images into the eye of the trooper, using his retina to produce the illusion of holographic images. The BSD also has a thermal viewing capability, which allows the user to see in the dark, and through smoke and haze, out to a range of two thousand meters. Finally, certain safeguards, such as oxygen activation, can be triggered by eye movement. At that speed, the BSD was in time to protect against the gas that erupted from the opening in the elevator.

"Sarin?" asked Sam.

"No," answered Sarah authoritatively. "This is worse than the Tokyo subways. Sarin gas would kill anyone in here now, but the lethality would take a long time to dissipate. There's no air flow, and no humidity in a cave. Unless they have a second elevator, they have to use this one, too, so Sarin's not a practical solution for them. I expect it's one of the standard anesthetics."

"And I expect there was some way of pressing the elevator button—a sequence of pushes, maybe at certain intervals—that intruders like us wouldn't know about," added Jennifer. "Miss that and you get the gas."

"So when this car reaches bottom, we're expected to be unconscious," said Hunter.

"Surprise!" chuckled Jack. He activated his Automatic Battlefield Motion Sensor and trained it on the doors in front of them.

The ABMS detects millimeter-wave changes in movement out to seven hundred meters and automatically alerts the trooper with a minor electric tingling sensation, in addition to a voice description of the threat and visual sensor information in the Battle Sensor Device. It's the equivalent of having a sixth sense.

The car made a small jerk and stopped. "Three to the left, three to the right," Jack reported happily, shifting to the left to train his Offensive Handgun Weapon System .45 Caliber Special Operations Forces Pistol to the right. Hunter and Sarah joined him, lining up beside him. Travis, Stan, and Jen reversed the procedure on the other side, while Sam stood back, the odd man out in this maneuver. "Activate your suits' camouflage," Travis ordered.

The doors began to slide open. The men waiting outside saw nothing in the car; they leaned forward to get a peek at the corners. And looked straight into six bullets. Jack, to the left of Hunter and Sarah, shot the Chinese guard on the right; Hunter shot the one in the middle; and Sarah, on the right, took the one on the left. Each member of TALON Force had an unobstructed shot as, across from them, Travis, Stan, and Jenny utilized the same maneuver.

The six shots were deafening in the enclosed area but that couldn't be helped. The thing now was to keep moving and find Wu.

Chapter 15

They came out into another large cavern, this one man-made. Again, the team saw evidence of the old scars of hand tools, but clearly the Triad had greatly enlarged and reworked what they found here. The cavern formed a rough corridor, running at least two hundred yards back. A number of doors, all closed, were set into the walls. The motion sensors showed movement behind three of the doors, all of it retreating. Soon there was no movement at all.

"Takin' out six at once shows we mean business and we're here in force," said Travis, his Texas twang more pronounced now in the adrenaline rush of battle. "They're not gonna confront us again unless they've got the odds in their favor."

"But they're not handing the place over to us," said Hunter.

"No. They're just regroupin', either to stage a counterattack or to let some other automatic defense mechanism get us."

"Look there," said Sam, pointing toward the ceiling. This time, instead of a gas nozzle, they saw a camera—then another, and another. He pulled out his OHWS Pistol, yelling, "My turn, darn it!" and shot out all three eyes.

"Lucky as always, Sambo," joked Jack.

"Now if they want to watch what we're doing, they'll have to come on down," Sam replied.

"Or get cable," smiled Jen.

They moved forward as a group toward the nearest door. Travis tried the knob and when it didn't turn, he blasted it off. The door swung drunkenly inward, revealing a room filled with weapons. There was nothing there that TALON needed; their own weaponry was far superior. Travis tossed an XM-17 Thermal Grenade inside, then quickly stepped back and pulled the door closed. They moved rapidly away as the heat began to explode the cartridges inside. For the next few minutes a fusillade was sounding, and bullets came flying through the door, ripping it to hunks, but most of the ammunition was contained in the stone room, ricocheting with hellish shrieks.

Other rooms revealed food caches, extra clothing and supplies, a barracks, and a mess hall. What they didn't reveal was any other inhabitants, including those they had heard running away. There didn't appear to be any way for the inhabitants to have left, nor any command center from where a Triad could be run.

"Stan, Hunter, Jack, Jen—there's got to be at last one secret exit. You and I will continue the search for it. Sarah, Sam—go through the personal effects of the men from the barracks—look for clues to Wu and his ultimate goal, and if you find that exit let us know."

On the alert for any new attack, the five went back toward the main underground cavern and began a more detailed search of the various rooms. The mess hall showed signs of long usage—the stove was heavily encrusted with grease, the dishwasher patched together with duct tape. The Ch'u Triad played for big stakes on the outside, but its men lived in the equivalent of battlefield conditions. Not such a bad approach, thought Travis. They feel they're a part of something monumental, but they don't lose their edge. Without that, it'd be tough to keep 'em holed up in this bunker

when Hong Kong's just down the road a piece. He
had to admire the Triad for that; they weren't just a
bunch of pretty gangbangers. But of course, if they
had been, they'd never have run afoul of TALON
Force.

The silence was beginning to get eerie. Travis re-
fused to believe that these guys just ran away and left
their bunker to an invasion force. Even if they knew
what TALON represented in terms of talent, they
seemed to outnumber the Americans and this was
their house.

"Look here, Trav!" Jen called from the food supply
room. The others came running.

She led them to the back wall. "All these rooms
are blasted out of solid rock. Makes it hard to hide
anything. But here we have an entire wall covered
with wooden shelving—with a wooden back."

"You think there's something behind it?"

In answer, she pointed at the stone floor. There had
been cardboard cartons of tea and sugar there, but
she'd pushed them aside to reveal curved scratches,
moving from the edge of the shelving outward.

"Stan, Jack—help me pull this thing out. If it won't
come easily we'll rip it down."

As the men moved forward, gunfire suddenly
erupted from the wall behind them, as well as the wall
across the room. It drove hard against their Battle
Ensembles, but the full Kevlar body armor they wore
beneath their suits reduced the impact to a rain of
hard thumps. The team members dived for cover, the
bullets nipping at their heels.

"Take 'em out!" snapped Travis, and they did. This
time, they activated their XM-29 Smart Rifles, to take
advantage of its armor-penetrating—in this case *stone*-
penetrating—ammunition. Precise shooting quickly reduced the hidden batteries to rubble.

"Very cleverly done," said Jen as she examined
what was left. "Automatic rifles, driven by more of
those cameras, so they can be aimed from afar. The

whole package was put in the wall and disguised with plaster, painted to look very close to the original rock. They could get away with it in two small spots, flanked by stand-alone shelving and other visual distractions."

"I don't mean to tell the camouflage expert her business," said Hunter, "but I think it's more than that. The scratches on the floor weren't really hidden that well—they only used cardboard boxes that could be easily moved. But when we tried to open the shelving there, we were right in the crossfire of the two guns."

"Stay on the alert," Travis told them. "We should've realized it after the trick with the elevator at the Finance building, but the Ch'u Triad likes tricks and misdirection."

"Anybody who succeeded at making a living in the no-man's-land between Hong Kong and the People's Republic, playing both ends against the middle, has to be trickier than the average bear," said Sam tartly through his mike.

"Well, keep it in mind. Have you found anything over your way?"

"A couple of grenades under some nasty old underwear," said Sarah. "Fortunately, bulges in men's underwear should always be handled with extreme prejudice, so we detonated 'em from a distance."

"You *always* have that effect on me, Sarah," said Sam, with a grin in his voice.

"All right, people," said Travis, "let's get our minds back in the game. We're gonna try to open a hidden door over here, so we may want you with us shortly."

"Just give the order, Travis," said Sarah.

The five turned back to the problem at hand. When Travis and Stan attempted to move the shelving, it bent outward at the top while the base remained solidly attached to the wall. Jen crouched and looked it over. After a moment she got up and left the room, returning from the mess hall with a long-handled knife. She knelt and probed with the blade, and before long there was a loud click. Six feet of the shelving pivoted away from the wall on hidden hinges, scraping along the stone floor.

Behind it was revealed another elevator door.

"Sam, Sarah, we've got a second elevator here. Stick with what you're doing while we check it out."

Travis pushed the single button beside the closed door, and the familiar hum began. After a moment, the door opened to reveal the car within.

"This one's a lot faster than the last one," said Jack.

"When you use this one, you've got places to go," said Hunter.

"You think there's gas in this one, too?" asked Stan.

"I'd bet on it," said Jen.

"Me, too," said Travis, looking the thing over with a critical eye. He stepped inside the waiting car.

Inside were two buttons, one above the other. The top one showed a glowing red light. "It seems to go down . . ." he said slowly. Abruptly, he turned and removed another small package from his Weapons Pak. It yielded two three-inch metal pads, which he slid onto his palms and secured with plastic straps. The pads generated a magnetic field, which could be turned on and off and enabled him to attach himself to metallic objects.

"What are you doing?" Stan asked.

"They like tricks. Let's see if they have any more in store for us. Go to oxygen."

The five went back on the self-contained atmosphere of the Battle Ensembles. Inside the elevator car, Travis removed his XM-29 Smart Rifle and jammed it across the open doorway to keep the door from closing. Then he moved his left hand toward the side wall. As it came near, the magnet was pulled strongly, slamming against the metal wall. Travis reached and pushed the bottom button with his right hand, then activated the right palm pad and let it adhere to the wall above the buttons.

The door tried to close and bounced back a few times—then suddenly the entire floor of the elevator car swung away on hidden hinges. The magnetic pads on Travis's palms prevented him from plummeting into the chasm.

He pulled himself up and placed his feet outside the car, back on solid rock. Then, by pressing a button at his fingertips, the pad loosened, enabling Travis to grab Stan's outstretched hand. He then disengaged his other hand and was pulled out of the car.

"What tipped you off?" Stan asked.

"Nothin' in particular. The whole setup," answered Travis. "I'm lookin' for traps everywhere now, and they'd already done gas in the outside elevator, and a bomb in the Ministry of Finance. What else might an enterprising group of psychos do with an elevator? I figured droppin' us down the shaft was a good possibility."

"How far down does it go?" wondered Jack.

"Let's find out," said Stan and took from his Pak the smallest of TALON's Hand-Launched Micro Unmanned Aerial Vehicles—the Dragonfly. It was roughly the same size as the palm magnets, but boasted a delta wing and rear-mounted propeller, enabling it to be incredibly maneuverable. It carried a microelectronics payload with the ability to see, making it the perfect vehicle for covert surveillance. For this mission, the team had also recently fitted it with a special "smelling" sensor, ostensively to pick up the presence of an odorless, colorless gas like Sarin. The Dragonfly could maneuver through small spaces like elevator shafts and look for hidden dangers using normal and night-vision sensors. But beyond that, it could sample the air as it went and, among other things, pick out the sweat or bad breath of men completely hidden from view.

Stan launched the Micro-UAV and sent it soaring through the bottomless elevator car and down the shaft. Each of the five flipped his Battle Sensor Device

eyepiece down over his left eye to see what the Dragonfly saw—except Jack, who turned toward the door
of the store room to keep an eye on their backs as
well.

The micro-plane descended in a tight spiral. Stan
used a small joystick to guide it down the shaft. One
level down, the Dragonfly saw the elevator door to
the next level, so there was, indeed, a positive use for
the elevator, besides the negative one of eliminating
intruders. Then, as the readout in their BSD's showed
a descent of twenty, forty, and finally fifty-two feet, it
reached running water. The unit's night-vision camera
revealed a broad expanse that ran sluggishly past the
bottom of the shaft, completely filling it.

"An underground river," said Stan.

"Probably leading to the Zhujiang—the 'Pearl' to
you," said Sam in his ear.

"What's your position, Sam?" asked Travis.

"Sarah and I are done in the barracks, and she re-
fuses to examine my underwear, so we're kickin' back
and watching TV."

"Forget your damn underwear and come on over
here."

"I do forget it, for weeks at a time. Us geeks, you
know . . ."

"I should never have mentioned it," moaned Sarah.
But the two separated members of TALON came on
the run as the team went back to discussing what
lay below.

"I imagine, besides carting away dead bodies, it
carts away all the other waste from this bunker," said
Hunter. "You know, shit and soap."

"Fifty-two feet straight down, then out the chute,"
said Jen. "A short but not-so-merry ride."

"By the time you—or what's left of you—winds up
in the Pearl River, you'll just be more crap from the
farmlands washing down to the South China Sea," said
Sam. "If there was anything left to identify, which I'm

betting there wouldn't be, there's no way anyone would ever track you back to here."

"So let's give the fifty-two-foot drop a pass and go for the door ten feet down instead," said Travis. "We can't use the magnets to climb down the rock, so we'll have to go for old-fashioned rappeling."

Stan brought the Micro-UAV back up and stowed it in his Pak while the others prepared for the descent. Travis and Hunter recovered a large hunk of rock blasted away from the wall in the weapons room and braced it across the front of the open elevator door. Cable was easily found in another of the Triad's rooms, and within five minutes they had tested its strength and were ready to descend.

"Stan, Hunter, you'll stay behind this time. If we flush troopers down there, they may well decide to cut off our retreat, and I'd prefer you don't let that happen."

"Ten-four," agreed Hunter laconically, but Stan protested.

"I don't like guard duty, Travis. I want to kick more butt!" He might have added, *And I don't want to be stuck with Hunter!*

"Unfortunately, Stan, you're only Number Two on this team," answered Travis good-naturedly. "As long as I'm in charge we'll do things my way, okay?"

Without waiting for an answer—which Stan was not foolish enough to offer in the first place—Travis turned his back to the elevator and began to rappel down the side.

Chapter 16

Ten feet down Travis braced his feet against the slight lip at the bottom of the elevator door and readied another thermal grenade. He pulled the pin and placed it on the lip, then counted to two before pushing off. He was at the outside arc of his swing when the grenade went off. As he came back in again, the others above pulled him upward so his feet touched above the melting door. He walked back up as the door disappeared below, with molten metal dripping into the river below. It made loud, echoing pops as it plopped into the cold water. He was not unhappy that his Battle Ensemble automatically adjusted its internal temperature, keeping him cool above the inferno of the grenade's blast.

Since he'd made certain of scrambling back to the floor above before anyone below could brave the thermal heat and stick a gun out to fire upward, Travis was somewhat surprised when nothing like that happened. The only sound from below was that of the melting metal crackling as it cooled. Stan deployed the Dragonfly again to have a look around on the lower floor and saw only more empty space.

"Those guys have got to be somewhere," he muttered. Then, brightening, he said, "Maybe they *will* try to come back this way."

With the Micro-UAV hovering inside the lower door, sending their Battle Sensor Devices a clear view of the empty chamber (as well as a readout of pure, clean air), the five began rappeling down the elevator shaft.

"Did any of you guys ever play any adventure games?" asked Sam. "I'm talking about the early days of personal computers, when the games were text-based. They were like Dungeons and Dragons, sort of, and you spent a lot of time wandering around passages in a cave or a pyramid or a haunted house. Zork was the original, on a mainframe at MIT."

"It's still there," said Sarah. "I played it when I was a student."

Sam turned to her enthusiastically. "You had to watch out not to get eaten by a Grue, and—"

"That'll do, Sam," said Travis.

"Yeah, let me know if you find a magic potion," Hunter joked.

The five were now on the lower floor. At a word from Travis, Stan flew his Dragonfly back upstairs, while Travis broke out one of his own. For the next five minutes, while silence reigned on all sides, the Micro-UAV flitted to all corners of the cavern. The cave appeared to be a smaller version of the one above, the primitive nature of its creation more evident. There were only two doors, one at each end, in addition to the elevator door.

"If they're not here then where the hell are they?" wondered Jen. "How many secret levels can they have?"

"Here's a thought," said Jack. "What if they just detonate this place and trap us down here?"

"I thought of that," said Travis. "But I don't believe they would. This is a hell of a base, in a country far less accepting of Triads than before the Hong Kong give-back. They're not going to write it off over seven invaders."

"Maybe they've been planning to relocate," suggested Jack.

"To where? Chinese crime gangs have moved to the West Coast of America and Canada, but they didn't outrage the world community by exploding Sarin bombs in a crowded city beforehand."

"Still," said Jen, "I'm getting tired of their doing nothing."

"Let me see if I can get an idea of what they're doing," said Sam. He dug into his Pak and came out with a small device the others didn't recognize. "This is a prototype of something I've been working on in my spare time," he said, with a touch of pride. "It's like what cable companies use to find cable pirates, only they need a truck for theirs. It picks up electromagnetic signals."

"Like the ones behind the cameras we've had aimed at us," said Sarah excitedly.

"Exactly."

He turned it on and tuned it a little, fiddling with a small dial. Soon a small red bulb on its upper surface lit up, flickered, and went out, then lit again . . . and stayed lit. "Electronics in there," Sam said, gesturing with the machine toward the door nearest them.

"Then let's check it out," grinned Jack and started forward.

"Wait," said Sam, and pointed at more cameras recessed in the ceiling on both sides of them. He then pointed his left fist at the door. On his wrist, as part of the Battle Ensemble, was a High Energy Radio Frequency device. The HERF generator was one of TALON's "nonlethal" weapons that used a short, intense burst of directed radio frequency energy to disable any piece of electronics with a computer chip. The HERF was woven right into the fighting ensemble and could be activated by voice command via the team's Micro-Biochip Transmitter/Receiver. After Sam activated his HERF, it sent a short, intense burst of radio frequency energy through the door. Inside the room there was a hollow metallic clang—like the sound a chair makes when it's tipped over by an occupant leaping up too fast.

The TALON five ran toward the door, double-time, and blasted it open. Inside was a small, squat, bald man, standing by an overturned chair, gaping with almost comic wonder at the smoke swirling from his bank of television monitors and computers.

"And this," said Sam, "is the Wizard of Oz."

As if finally realizing his situation, the man abruptly tried to dodge past the five and escape through the door. A rabbit in a rattlesnake den would have had a better chance. Jack and Travis wrapped him up and he struggled momentarily before accepting his fate. Three Offensive Handgun Weapon System .45 Caliber Special Ops Pistols and two 9mm Barettas appeared before his face.

"So," said Sam in Cantonese, "where are the rest of your people?"

"Fuck you!"

"Now, now. That won't get you anywhere."

"You destroyed my machines."

"Yeah, well, I know how you feel, but you *were* trying to kill us with them."

"This is my place, not yours!"

Sam made a sour face. "And Tokyo was the place of sixteen hundred people who are no longer alive, thanks to you and your buddies. So what did you expect?"

"You can kill me, but I'll never talk."

"That's what your buddy in Tokyo said, before he told us all about this place." Sam's characteristic easygoing banter was nowhere in evidence now. His eyes were as cold as the stone all around them. "I think you should accept the fact that you *will* talk if we put our minds to it, and we would like nothing better than to do that. The Ch'u Triad is way out of its league this time, and it is going to pay. We are going to make it pay. Are we clear?"

At the iron tone in Sam's voice, the little man appeared to wilt. Sam was short and skinny and funny-looking, but his affinity for the cold logic of computers could turn his voice just as frigid and unyielding. The belligerence drained from their prisoner's face, replaced by something close to awe. The little man looked around at the five people in Battle Ensembles crowding him and gave it up. "What do you want?"

"Where are the rest of your people?"

"Down—down another level. You won't tell them I talked, will you?"

"That depends on you. How do we get below?"

"There's another elevator, just for this level and that one. Each level is only connected with the level above and the level below, using separate elevators."

"Where is the elevator that goes down?"

"I'll show you."

"Do it."

Sam translated what they'd said while the little man, shivering now, led them back into the main chamber and to the other room. Inside, it appeared to be a filing area, with rows and rows of cabinets, stocked with sheaves of dossiers. Travis looked at it and whistled. "It'd be a shame to let this fall into Beijing's hands before Washington has a chance to study it. We'll have to work out a little moving party, after we finish up with the guys below."

The little man moved to two cabinets, each three feet across and six feet high.

"Do you feel lucky, punk?" asked Sam in Cantonese.

"What?" The little man was confused.

"If there's a booby trap involved in this, you won't live to see it play out."

"Booby trap? No, not this far down." The man placed his hands between the cabinets and pulled them apart. Though they looked as if they weighed a thousand pounds each, they slid apart easily on hidden bearings. Behind them was another elevator door.

"You run it," said Travis.

The little man pushed the single button three times, then twice, then twice again. The sound of the motor engaging reached them, and in a moment the door slid wide.

"Inside."

The little man entered willingly enough; each member of TALON Force was watching for signs of anything awry. Still, each took one of their magnetic pads and clamped onto an elevator wall before continuing.

"Take us down."

The little man pressed the lower of the interior buttons and the car began to descend. Suddenly Sam noticed the little man tensing up. "Travis, this guy's got some game going," he began—then they were all struck by a sensation TALON Force knew too well. It was a the sickening feeling induced by a nonlethal generator. An NLG emits a low-frequency radio field which first disorients its victim and then makes him violently ill. TALON had them in their own arsenal and had trained against them. The Battle Ensemble was designed to shield them from it. This signal was much stronger than their Battle Ensembles could deflect. The last thing any of them saw was the little man quivering like a gut-shot dog. Then all was pain and blessed darkness.

Chapter 17

Stan and Hunter were on opposite sides of the food storage room, each halfway between the elevator and the entrance door, when they were jolted by a disembodied voice speaking in accented English.

"Americans! We have your five compatriots."

Stan stood bolt upright, straining to discover where the voice had come from. "Yeah, and I know an honest politician."

"If you go to the barracks area, you'll find a television. Tune it to channel 99."

The two looked at each other across the room. Without a word between them, they made their way to the door out of the room and pressed their backs against the wall on either side. Stan went out first, with a rush, his XM-29 Smart Rifle ready. When he was satisfied that no one was waiting for them, he alerted Hunter. Heads low, they jogged to the barracks and entered it with the same military precision they'd left the pantry. It, too, appeared deserted as they crossed the room, but they still kept a vigilant watch for traps.

Still nothing. So Stan flipped on the TV and dialed the channel.

The image that appeared was a still-camera shot of their five teammates, minus their Battle Ensembles, bound and apparently unconscious, in a featureless stone room.

The television spoke: "As you see, I'm not lying. Your combat suits are impressive, but insufficient to defeat the Ch'u Triad. Now, you will return to the pantry and make your way to the lower level, where you will be given further instructions."

"You would be Mr. Wu, I take it," said Stan.

"That's right. And if it will feed your egos at all, I am amazed that you found me here. But the Ch'u Triad has had many years to design our 'hideout' and we did not embark on our present course without making certain we were as strong as we could possibly be."

"And what would that present course be? You didn't get anything out of gassing defenseless Japanese."

"In point of fact, we Chinese get a great deal out of killing Japanese—or are you too young to have heard of the Second World War? But your larger point is true: we have bigger plans."

"That's why we came, Wu. To have you tell us what they are."

"Then I'll make certain to tell you nothing. This is not an American film. Once you join your friends under my control, you'll find I will not gloat and tell you everything you want to know." Wu's voice suddenly lost its urbane geniality. "No! You will just die!"

"Then I think we'll pass on your offer," said Stan. "Personally, I'd rather fight my way back to the surface."

"Go right ahead. Reinforcements from Hong Kong have arrived and already occupy the outer cave. If—if—you could get there, you would certainly die. And you wouldn't get there because the elevator is fully prepared to stop you. I remind you to look at the television. You see that you can't withstand us."

"I'd still rather die fighting—"

Hunter clapped a hand on Stan's shoulder. "Wait," he said.

"What are you, surrendering?" snapped Stan, glaring up at him.

This time Hunter spoke on their com channel through the Battle Sensor Helmet. "I have an idea, Stan!"

For ten seconds the two men stood there, apparently silent.

"No more stalling!" snarled Mr. Wu. "Go down or attempt to go up, but go now or your friends will die sooner than expected."

Stan raised his head. "I want to talk with my commander when we get there."

"I make no deals, American. Go!"

Stan gave Hunter a very hard look, then the two men left the room. They stood in the central chamber and Stan looked hard at the elevator leading upward, but Hunter tugged on his shoulder, pulling him toward the pantry.

They went to the elevator and looked into the shaft. The cable leading to the floor below was still there.

"I hope you've got your head screwed on straight, Richie Rich!" said Stan.

"We'll find our, pygmy," said Hunter and managed a grin. "Just for laughs, I'll go first."

He squatted beside the opening, grabbed the cable, and started to rappel downward. Stan was right behind him. His helmeted head had just disappeared below the doorway when he suddenly shouted, "Oh, shit!"— and both men plummeted straight down the empty shaft into the cold, dark river.

Chapter 18

"What happened?" Mr. Wu was normally a man who prided himself on his self-control, but right now he was almost hopping with fury. The younger man beside him at the television monitor bank had no answer.

"The cable must have broken," he ventured. "We have no camera in the elevator shaft, but the way they disappeared from the second level—I'm sure I saw them fall past the third level opening."

"Perhaps they're trying to escape out the river."

"Does it matter? It can't be done. The river runs through a tangled passage for over seven miles, in some places narrowing to less than a foot. Their suits are state-of-the-art, but even with an oxygen supply and explosives, they can't make it. Preliminary analysis of their companions' suits indicates an oxygen supply much too limited for a journey that long."

"It *does* matter, Xiang, because I wanted to kill them myself. Seven highly trained commandos, two of them women—I could have fulfilled very long-held fantasies."

"You still have five, sir. And you have their battle suits."

"Five is not seven, and suits are not men."

When Stan and Hunter hit the water of the underground river, they were ready. In the ten seconds

Hunter had talked with Stan through their Micro-Bio-chip Transmitter/Receiver, he'd said enough to make his idea clear.

"The Dragonfly smelled shit and soap in the river. That means it's being used as their sewer. *That* means there are pipes running down to—*and up from*—the river . . ."

Of course, what he hadn't said—hadn't needed to say—was that if they dived fifty-two feet and the river was shallow at that point, they were dead men. But they'd both seen what the Dragonfly had seen down there, and the water appeared to be moving the way deeper water does. It afforded a chance, which was enough at that point. TALON Force did not leave anyone behind. All seven were coming out, or none of them were. So if Stan and Hunter died in the river it was no different from dying while fighting their way to the surface, or getting killed when the Triad came to get them in the barracks.

So they went to the pantry and climbed down the cable—and let go.

The black water surged around them as they hit the surface. A fifty-foot dive was nothing for a trained athlete, and their Battle Ensembles took the brunt of the blow anyway. The ensembles also instantly adjusted their temperatures to counteract the shock of the cold water. And even as the men were falling, they'd flicked their eyes to activate oxygen and the thermal viewing capacity of the Battle Sensor Devices in their helmets. The BSDs let them see out to two thousand meters in the dark, through smoke, haze, and now water. So instead of being fifty feet down a dark shaft in dark water, the world they encountered was as wide as a river and reasonably illuminated in a sharp green light.

"You alive?" asked Hunter through the Micro-Bio-chip Transmitter/Receiver.

"Yeah."

"Damn. I was hoping I'd be rid of you."

"No such luck, Cube. Now switch this frequency to include just us two. With the other suits in enemy hands, I don't want them finding out how lame you are."

"Done."

"Outstanding. So—this was your idea. Now what?"

"Now we swim upstream."

"Easy for me. Maybe not so much for you."

"Just don't get caught in my wake, pygmy."

They took one last look upward, then dived and began searching for an opening. It was another ten feet down, a jagged gash in the cave rock. The current there was much stronger because of the elevated water pressure in the passageway behind it; only when the river could expand into the man-made shaft did it lose some of its momentum. So the closer the two men got to the opening, the harder the water pushed them away.

They swam past the sides of the gash to settle in below it. The water tended to rush upward so the current was weaker down there. They then worked their way crablike across the rock face, clinging to the slightest handholds, until they were finally next to the opening. They could still see fine with their thermal-viewing capacity, but what they saw was the bubbling swirl of water rushing from a hole. There was no way to know what was inside.

"I'll pull myself in," said Stan. "Hand over hand. Once I get to where I can use my feet, I'll brace myself across the passage and you can use me to pull yourself in."

"I'll push your feet as best I can."

No use wondering if the gash was too wide inside to allow that. It either was or it wasn't.

Stan took a deep breath and hurled himself into the maelstrom. His right hand grabbed for a handhold and missed and he flew backward out of the opening, somersaulting over Hunter.

Shaking his head grimly, Stan caught himself in the

water and came back for a second try. This time when he surged inside, he grabbed to the left and caught an outcropping. It was smooth from centuries of the polishing effect of rushing water, but Stan's strong fingers kept their grip. He stabbed out with his right hand and slammed his fingers into an unseen rock, lucky not to have broken something. But he wrapped his throbbing fingers around the rock and established a purchase inside the hole.

Hand over hand, he pulled himself forward. At last he could brace his knees against the stone. Then, finally, his feet were inside. He waited and felt Hunter grab his right ankle, then proceeded. For five more minutes he crawled along blindly. Somewhere during that time Hunter was far enough inside to let go and do his own crawling. But here was one place where being the short guy worked to Stan's benefit. The tall pilot would have to follow as best he could.

The passage began to descend and narrow. The speed of the water increased. The readout before his left eye from the BSD indicated just fourteen minutes of oxygen left . . . when all at once, the passage opened upward into a huge calm cavern.

Stan swam up into it and looked around. It was a natural cave filled with water, extending more than two thousand meters. Except for the vicious suction at the bottom where the passageway to the shaft opened—and, no doubt, at the point where the river entered—this chamber was almost perfectly calm. Swimming in it was like being in outer space, drifting in a void.

Below, Hunter was struggling out of the opening and soon came up to join him. Stan directed his attention to the ceiling. There, some thirty meters away, was an opening about four feet across, and even as they watched, some nasty-looking material floated down out of it.

The two men looked at each other. "Now I know

how those alligators in the New York sewers feel," said Stan.

"Just so long as you keep going first," said Hunter. "But see, with so many men in this bunker, on so many levels, I knew the sewer pipe would have to be a big one."

Stan swam up toward the opening. Since it was a disposal pipe it was completely open; there was nothing obstructing its mouth. By pressing outward with his hands and then his knees, Stan was able to shinny up inside. At first the climb was relatively easy, but when, after twelve feet, he reached the air, he found that the slime coming down the pipe for years had coated the metal with a thick, slippery goo (and "goo" was the only word Stan could bear to give it). Fortunately, the pipe *was* metal, so after he flicked off his oxygen supply he braced himself inside the pipe's confines while he slipped on his magnetic pads.

After that it was simply a matter of spidering up the pipe and suffering the slop that occasionally washed down on their heads. Hunter, mostly blocked by Stan above him, made sure to laugh every time. For his own part, Stan, growing accustomed to the sound of flushing echoing from above, did his best to get out of the way and let it go by him to land on Hunter.

But there was a sense of real urgency about this maneuver. The water-filled cavern had been significantly below the bottom of the elevator shaft, so the climb upward took some time—time that their five teammates in the hands of their enemies did not have. They knew they only had to get to the lowest level, but there was no telling how far that would be. After a few more minutes of climbing, Stan finally saw what he'd been searching for above him: an opening in the side of the pipe. That would be where the plumbing in the lowest level connected with the main pipe. And as he reached that opening, he heard voices echoing far away like ghosts.

He used the Micro-Biochip. "Hey, rich boy."

"Yeah, pygmy."

"We're here. I'm gonna try communicating with the others."

"If they're not wearing their helmets you can only talk line-of-sight, and the only line of sight here contains your ass."

"I know, but I'd like to alert them to our presence if I can. It's worth the risk."

He changed the frequency with the flick of his eye and said, cautiously, "Travis. This is Stan and Hunter."

There was no answer.

Stan shut down the transmission and switched back to Hunter only. "They're not responding. Must be out of range—or still out of the suits. I think we should stop lollygaggin' around."

"My thoughts exactly."

"All right then. I'm gonna blow a hole in the wall here. It won't be subtle but it'll be effective. The only problem is the impact of the sound on our ears in this enclosed space. Best we can do is place the explosive as far inside the cross-pipe as possible, then climb above it and use the bulk of our bodies to block the sound."

"So let's do it."

Stan pried an XM17 Thermal Grenade from his Pak, then another for good measure. Holding one in each hand, he crawled forward into the side pipe. It went on for only ten feet before it made the over-under wave curve all drainage systems have in common. That meant the toilets were right above his head. He lovingly placed the grenades together and rather than pull the rings, he turned them clockwise. This allowed the grenades to be detonated on a radio signal. He scraped the "goo" from the pipe walls and packed it around the XM17s, then backed out into the main vertical pipe. Hunter was already above him.

"Thought I'd put you in front of me when the bomb went off," said Stan, climbing to meet him.

"I know you did, Stan, but the day hasn't dawned when a Navy guy can outthink the Air Force."

Stan got into place, and both men turned to position their butts toward the blast point. They huddled over, placing their heads between their drawn-up legs, pressing their knees against their ears. Stan brought up the detonation screen on his BSD.

"Three, two, one," he said and flicked his eye—

The blast ripped through the air, assaulting them. The pipe seemed to swell with it, and both troopers skidded down the sides for a moment. And when the scathing heat and pounding shock was over, a tremendous ringing still reverberated through the pipe and in their shocked ears. But Stan and Hunter, on the move, were already skidding back down the pipe and into the side passage. Ahead there was no longer darkness. Now there was light, and smoke, and a severed leg.

Stan and Hunter burst up out of what had once been a three-stall bathroom but was now a heap of rubble. The man without a leg was missing most of the rest of him, too, his remains lying sprawled across a crooked sink. The other man, whom Stan had heard him talking to, lay just outside the room, his arms flopping but his legs ominously still below a badly broken back.

The two TALON Force troopers picked their way through the shambles, exiting the bathroom and bursting into a large operations room, elaborately outfitted with high-tech gear. Another communications control center was visible through an open door. A room with what looked like a golden door, closed, was next to it. At the end of the cavern was an elevator, and beside that was a room with a barred prison door. Two more closed doors marked the near wall.

Most importantly, the cavern itself was beginning to fill with Triad troops with AK-47s, pouring lead in their direction.

Stan and Hunter dove for cover behind the smoldering heaps of stone and porcelain, their XM-29 Smart Rifles gliding into position against their shoulders as naturally as their breathing.

The XM-29 Smart Rifle, when fully utilized, fired special smart bullets that were directed by a millimeter-wave sensor and aiming device located beneath the barrel. The device automatically locked onto hard targets and made minor adjustments to direct the bullets with deadly precision. Each XM-29 carried a basic load of fifty rounds of 4.55mm ammo in the box magazine near the trigger. But when your bullets know where to go and can penetrate most bulletproof vests, fifty is a lot more than you'll generally need. In this case it took just twelve shots between the TALON troopers to down the eleven Chinese. In less than half a minute the cavern was secured.

Chapter 19

"None of those guys was Wu," said Stan. Hunter, his ears still ringing from the grenade blast, could barely make his words out.

"I'll open the cell," he said. "Cover me."

Hunter ran across the cavern, alert for the slightest movement from any of the closed doors, and flattened himself against the wall beside the communications doors, and flattened himself against the wall beside the communications room. "On three," he said to Stan through the Micro-Biochip. "One—two—"

Stan raked the wall above the door with conventional fire to drive anyone inside the room back, and a split second afterward Hunter dashed across the open doorway. Shots from inside followed him but too late; he reached the far side of the doorway without incident.

"*There's* Mr. Wu," he said.

Stan shouted across the cavern as Hunter moved on toward the cell, "No place to go, Wu! We've given your hellhole the complete termite inspection, and there ain't no fourth level. So come on out quietly or we'll show you what other high-tech goodies we've got up our sleeves."

Wu shouted back from inside the room, "And I'll show you what I have! You'll never enter this room!"

"You don't get it, Wu!" yelled Hunter. "We don't have to get in there to lay you out like your troopers!"

There was silence from inside. Then, "You said you needed my information!" Wu shouted.

It would have been nice to think that Wu was considering surrender, but neither of the TALON men was that easily fooled. Wu was the Number Two man in the Triad so he had to have guts, and he had shown himself to be too fond of command when he'd thought he'd had them in *his* power before.

"We don't *need* your information, Wu. We'll take it if we can get it, but it won't buy you anything." That last was a lie, but there was no sense giving the guy any leverage.

Hunter ran to the cell door and pulled out one of his XM17 Thermal Grenades.

"I might be persuaded to tell you what you want to know," shouted Wu, a tremor of uncertainty in his voice. "It's about our final plan, isn't it? I'll come out if you give me your word you won't hurt me. If you let me walk away afterward, we can make a deal. You've destroyed my operation here so I don't care what happens to the plan now, and the rest of them can go—"

"Hunter!" Stan bellowed.

Hunter's body jerked in response. "I'm right here, Stan. Cool off."

"No, you cool off. Mr. Wu is talking way too much, and I remember what Travis said about the Triad's trickery. Don't touch that damn cell. Let's have him do it."

Calling across the cavern once again, Stan said, "Wu, I'm giving you till five to come out with your hands up. After that I get to remove you any way I want to."

Wu's voice no longer carried a tremor when he answered, coldly, "I think not."

"It's your call."

Stan pulled out his Micro-UAV again and turned to wink at Hunter before running across the cavern to the wall beside the open door. Hunter covered him, jogging to the far side for a better angle. Stan launched the Dragonfly, directing it into the communications room. They both watched through their BSDs' video-imaging displays as it came in low and fast and spun into a tight spiral. Three-quarters of the way around it locked on Wu, half-hidden behind a projection television screen. Wu snapped off a shot from a Glock and the image went black, but the Micro-UAV had served its purpose. Stan and Hunter, knowing his exact location, activated their Low Observable Camouflage Suites, and their images shivered into invisibility. Like the Dragonfly, they, too, went in low and fast, seeking cover as their Automatic Battlefield Motion Sensors picked up Wu immediately, alerting the soldiers in a soft voice: "Hard target acquired, two point four meters ahead." They crouched among the computer banks and television monitors that would afford protection from any wild shots.

Wu looked around uncertainly, the Glock tight in his hand. He had caught a glimpse of fluid movement as they entered. He had heard their boots on the stone floor. But he couldn't tell where they were. That might have unnerved a lesser man right there. But Wu's face showed a renewed determination.

Stan and Hunter moved toward him, a bit at a time. They couldn't risk killing him without getting his information, and the clutter of the communications room made a clear shot difficult. Still, with each man moving a foot or three at a time, at times when Wu was looking in the wrong direction, they were closing in with deadly efficiency.

And then Wu shot Stan just underneath his outstretched arm.

Stan went down, crashing into the computers, and Wu swung his pistol toward Hunter, but by then Hunter was all over him. With three moves he put Wu on the floor and sent his pistol skidding to the wall. But the gang lord was tough and quick reflexes guided him to fight back. Though Hunter was still invisible, Wu could feel enough of Hunter at this range to know where to throw his punches if he aimed for the torso, and he threw them hard. The two men reeled around the room smashing the sparking equipment. Hunter's size and strength almost complimented Wu's wiry stamina and drive. But at last Wu made a mistake. He aimed a punch at the spot he thought Hunter's head must be and missed it altogether. For one moment he was completely vulnerable, and Hunter didn't miss it. He hammered Wu in the kidneys, and before the gang lord could recover, Hunter landed a crushing blow to his spine. Now Wu was just trying to hang on, and mere grappling was no strategy against a TALON trooper with a mean on. Two more blows from Hunter to the jaw and the back of the neck, and Wu was down and out.

Hunter quickly tied Wu's hands behind him with a plastic restraint, then finally was able to get to Stan's side. To save power, his eye flicked off his suit's invisibility, then did the same for Stan, manually. His friend was down but not out. He even had a smile on his face.

"Well, *damn* rich boy," said Stan. "Never saw that side of you. Where'd you learn that, prep school?"

"Where'd he get you?"

"High up. Clipped my arm pit. But I don't think he hit anything that won't heal."

Hunter examined the wound and saw Stan was right. The Battle Ensemble had Biochip Health Status Sensors built in throughout the suit. These sensors continuously monitored vital body functions, and when necessary directed the immediate closure of any puncture wounds through brilliant fibers within the ensemble. Then they activated lifesaving drugs and fluids from the Automatic Medical Trauma Pack, also embedded in the ensemble. The ATMP could deal with 76 percent of all battlefield wounds, so long as they weren't catastrophic.

By now Stan was feeling no pain. With his blood loss stabilized and the wound already on the mend, he'd be able to evacuate under his own power.

"Remind me to play some high-stakes poker with you when we get back," said Hunter. "You must be the world's unluckiest guy to get hit while you're invisible."

"There was no luck involved. He *knew* where we were."

"How? He couldn't see us."

"Hunter, we just crawled up a sewer. He *smelled* us."

Hunter gave him a puzzled look, then sniffed the air. He then fell back on his haunches, laughing. "You're right! I must have completely blocked it out! It was so bad it interfered with my ability to function!"

"I guess Wu's sensibilities are a little bit more refined than yours, uptown boy." Then they both dissolved into laughter again—even as Hunter kept a close and approving eye on Stan's condition.

Finally, Hunter stood up. "You ready to get our buddies out?"

"I was born ready," said Stan. "I don't think I'll be carrying anything heavy from here on in—unless I have to—but I'm right with you." Stan got up smoothly, though he couldn't hide a certain light-headedness. Hunter decided he didn't need to worry about him anymore.

He walked over and kicked Wu in the side. "Get up, you bastard. You've got a cell to open."

Wu rolled over with a theatrical groan. "I'm . . . I'm hurt."

"Christ, can't you do anything without bullshitting me? Get up or I'll show you exactly what hurt is."

"I'll need help, with my hands tied behind my back."

"You'll get thirty seconds to do it yourself. You shot my partner, Wu; your time for favors is long gone."

Wu rolled to his side and drew his knees up, then flopped back over with his nose to the ground. He awkwardly got his feet underneath him and lurched to a standing position. He almost toppled over, but knowing no one was going to catch him, he fought to stay upright and won.

"Now then, Wu, I'm not going to ask you if you've got any more tricks or troops down here, because that would be a waste of time. But I can *tell* you that from now on, you're going to do what we say, or we'll make you wear your ass for a hat. You dig?"

"Eh?"

"Good. Now, where are our teammates?"

"In the cell."

"Then you're going to open it."

"As you say." The Triad leader showed no sign of emotion now, appearing resigned. But his lax demeanor could mean that he could snap at any minute. Hunter had little choice but to stay close to him inside this madhouse of traps.

Chapter 20

They went out into the central cavern, Stan sweeping his XM-29 stiffly behind the others. Hunter adjusted the bonds on Wu, twisting his left arm tightly up behind his back and looping another plastic strap around his wrists so that any struggle would make the ties tighter. Then he secured another strap between Wu's ankles, efficiently hobbling him.

The two TALON members took up positions on either side of the chamber and sent Wu toward the barred doors of the cell. Wu moved across the stone floor like a man with his pants around his ankles and used his free right hand to fiddle with the electronic panel beside the door. After a minute the door popped open with a muffled whoosh—and the rest of the team filed out, unarmed but prepared to fight. They'd been stripped of their Battle Ensembles and were wearing only combat fatigues. When they saw the chamber littered with Wu, eleven dead Triads, and a blasted bathroom, they came to a surprised but appreciative halt.

Jen pinched her nose. "You guys smell like—"

"We know, we know," said Hunter.

"Is that a bullet wound, Stan?" Travis asked quietly.

"He tried for my heart. Didn't know I don't have one."

"You okay?"

"At the moment I don't feel a thing. Automatic Trauma Meds work like a charm. Here." He tossed his XM-29 to Jack with just a small grimace. "Make yourself useful, gyrene. Check out those two closed doors for rodents."

"Sorry, Trav. I tried to lose him on the way," said Hunter, as Jack moved smartly to comply, "but Stan has a knack for sticking to your skin."

"I hate to think what else is stuck there," said Sarah, going over to examine Stan's wound and making sure the ATMP was monitoring his vitals the way it was supposed to.

Travis turned to the captive. "This Wu?"

"In the all-too-ugly flesh," said Hunter. "Him I'd like to lose permanently, but we haven't had an opportunity to hear him sing yet."

"I will tell you nothing," snapped Wu.

"That's what your com chief upstairs said, before you killed him in the elevator," said Jack. "Tell me this, Wu—did he know what was going to happen to him?"

"Absolutely." The thought brought a cruel smile to Wu's face. "He was loyally trained, if captured, to lead his captors into that elevator and await the honor that bringing death to one's enemies bestows."

Jack nodded. That's the way he would have done it, too. Jack appreciated the code of killing, but he also recognized the difference between loyalty and brainwashing. "These rooms are empty, Travis. But our Battle Ensembles and weapons are here."

"So we've got the place all to ourselves?"

"Wu says reinforcements have moved into the original cave up top," Hunter said.

"Is there any other way out, besides that elevator?" Travis asked, motioning toward the metal door.

"No. I wouldn't take Stan back the way we came—"

"—and if we did go that way, we couldn't get back up the elevator shaft," Stan cut in. "The cable didn't reach far enough down. The only option would be to go on downstream, but I don't like the odds."

"No," said Travis. "In fact, Wu regaled us with stories of your tortured deaths after you disappeared into the river. He said you'd come out the far end as hamburger. He was actually pretty pissed that he wouldn't get to do to you what he planned to do to us."

"Which was?"

"Oh, he hadn't gotten around to it yet, so I guess we'll never know." Travis turned to Wu. "But we *will* need to know what your gang has planned for the grand finale."

"I will tell you nothing."

"You will. You just want to buy time. And as it happens, you win that round for now. We don't *have* the time to work on you while we're still down here and the friends you invited could burst in at any moment. But I want you to think about this: when we do have the chance to pry you open, we're gonna be a lot more direct than we might've been otherwise."

Wu sneered.

Travis yelled at Jack, "Collect the Battle Ensembles. We're on our way."

The five donned their TALON suits, and Travis insisted each run a full diagnostic; he was not going to suffer any more surprises from Triad tricks if he could help it. The suits checked out fine. The rescue had come too quickly for Wu's crew to dismantle them.

When they were ready, Travis confronted the elevator. "We'll go up in groups of two, with Wu and me along for all the rides. So if anything happens, it happens to him, too. He was willing to play that game with his underlings but I doubt he'll play it with himself; if he does, the rest of you'll have to try something else. Just so's you know"—he turned to Hunter and Stan—"he's got a Nonlethal Generator in there."

"Punch the button, Wu," ordered Hunter. The Triad chieftain hobbled to the elevator and complied, using a sequence of one-one-five.

The elevator door opened. Travis motioned Sarah and Stan to enter with him. "Let's see if our Wristband RF Field Generator can take out the NLG," he said. The three of them pointed their left wrists at the elevator ceiling and activated the RFFG. Then they swept the field down the sides and finally raked the floor with it, careful not to hit the control banks. "I don't know where it's attached, and there's no guarantee we can kill it—we have no idea how thick this metal is."

"C'mon, Wu." The Chinese gang lord lurched into the car and punched the "up" button. The door slowly closed, the hum of the motor began, and the car started to rise. The four TALON members left behind waited until the car reappeared.

When the door opened again, it revealed Travis with his .45 to Wu's temple inside. "Jen, Jack." And after they'd gone, the car came back for Hunter and Sam. Soon they were reassembled on the second level, without incident.

The next stop proceeded just as smoothly. Travis asked Wu for the code to run the elevator with the floorless hatch, and got an answer, which he then tested. The floor of the car swung upward and shut as the car came down to their level. Again the trip upward was accomplished in three groups.

Finally they took a moment to ready themselves for the ascent to the surface. They would have to go up in force to face the new cavalry, so they activated their suits' invisibility and piled in. Wu—now apparently the only one there—punched a sequence on the "up" button.

The ride was smooth and quick. They came to a halt and the door slid open. The team came out combat-ready, but the surface cavern showed no signs of living human habitation; the dead humans who had defended the cave in the first place were scattered where they'd fallen. It was perfectly conceivable that living soldiers were playing dead among the corpses, waiting for the moment to leap up and begin fighting. But Travis had an answer for that. The team's Automatic Battlefield Motion Sensor detected millimeter-wave changes in movement. As the group made its way through the cave, they detected no motion from any of the bodies.

But ahead was the exit into the open field. Wu's reinforcements could be behind the trees on the far side of the clearing, or, more likely, hidden among the rocks on the hill above the opening. The ABM sensor couldn't see through rocks and the trees were too far away, so the only way to find out was to get out of the cave. Once that happened, the Triad forces wouldn't be able to see the TALON members. But in the midst of TALON was the perfectly visible Wu.

"Travis," said Hunter. "Let's put Mr. Wu to sleep and leave him here while we secure the area."

"I thought of that," answered Travis. "But we need his information. I don't like letting him out of my sight."

"I'll stay with him," said Sam.

"No, I may need you for translations."

"I'll do it," Stan said. "I may not be up for running around in a firefight, but I'm good to sit on my ass and watch this customer."

"You're always good to sit on your ass," said Travis with a smile. "All right. The rest of you people—we've got a job to do."

Travis and his team burst from the cave mouth, spreading out as if bullets were whistling around their heads. But the only sound was the midsummer drone of insects. Hunter, Jen, and Sam ran toward the trees on the far side of the field, eyes intently scanning for snipers. Travis, Sarah, and Jack stopped after ten yards and whirled back toward the overhanging hillside. They immediately saw movement among the rocks and alerted the others. In response, Hunter and Jen held their positions in the field but turned back to face the rocks. Sam kept his eyes on the trees as a precaution.

Now there were five TALON troopers peering up at the hillside, counting at least twenty men behind the boulders. The Triad force was antsy, waiting for their prey to emerge from the cave, and thinking they were as yet unseen, they made little attempt to hide.

"It's like watching the audience through a hole in the curtain," said Jennifer, the actress, on the transmitter.

"Let's bring the curtain up," answered Travis. "Everyone except Sam, move right up next to the rocks and spread out. And Jack—"

"Yeah, boss?"

"Leave any rattlesnakes alone."

The reinforcements from the Ch'u Triad were wondering what the hell was going on. They'd been rushed in from Hong Kong as if a great emergency were in progress, but when they got here they'd had no further orders. It didn't occur to them that there was no one left inside the bunker to give orders. Undoubtedly, Mr. Wu was engaged in a project and as soon as he was ready, he would radio and tell them what he wanted done. And there wasn't a man on the hillside who was going to question that. Still, they hadn't had any breakfast, nor had they packed any rations. They expected to come do their duty and either die or get it done, and then visit the bunker's mess hall. Whereas now, they were sitting in the July sun, leaning against hot rocks, and not a goddamn thing was happening.

Five shots sounded and the five men farthest forward kicked backward with blood streaming from their heads.

Stunned, the rest of the Triad force instinctively ducked for cover, and from that cover rained answering fire toward the bottom of the hill. But it soon petered out when they realized that there was no one there to fire upon.

"Snipers?" bawled the second-in-command to his leader.

"Can't be. The shots were too loud to have come from the trees."

"Then the attackers must be right behind the front rocks," yelled a man on the far left. "I didn't see them. Did you?"

There was a small chorus of "no."

"But they have to be there. They have to have reached over the tops of the rocks and fired."

"Flank them," shouted the leader. "Pin them in a crossfire."

Men on the left and right moved out, crawling on elbows and knees down the hill behind the rocks. Dust filled their noses. After the moment of complete confusion, it helped them to know where the enemy was. But the Triad men were keeping well-covered until they saw the bastards for themselves.

The remaining troops peered down at the rocks that had to be hiding their attackers. Their eyes grew tired from the intensity of it, and the mid-morning heat caused the air to shimmer. Faint images a man could mistake for human drifted away from the rocks.

The first Chinese reached the point where they'd be able to see their enemies. But there was nothing to see. They crawled a bit forward. Still nothing. Their comrades farther up the hill held their breath and waited for the moment when firing would erupt.

It soon indeed erupted, and the men at the bottom of the hill jerked and died.

"Ghosts!" screamed the second-in-command, and loosed a stream of lead at the side of the hill, where it seemed to him the newest shots had come from. His men joined him, shooting at thin air, not sure if they believed in ghosts but very sure that their lives were in grave danger.

Before they calmed down, they'd accidentally killed three more of their own.

Now there were only eight members of the Triad

left alive. They couldn't make any sense of what was happening to them. But their leader knew one thing for certain: they had been called to fight an emergency involving the cave. Whatever was wrong, it originated from there. "Rush the cave!" he yelled. If nothing else, it might provide them shelter.

His remaining men were happy to have any goal now. They leapt to their feet and charged. They didn't care that they were abandoning their cover; what good had cover done them so far? And as they fully expected, bullets from invisible enemies started firing from both the left and right. But the Chinese men were running down a rock-strewn hillside. They sped up, they slowed down, they dodged and leapt. They were not easy targets. Of the eight men who started down the hill, two reached the bottom.

One was the leader. He hit the field's grass and spun toward the dark opening. A bullet sang past his ear and for the first time he saw a living person! Unfortunately, it was Mr. Wu. By the time he realized that, he'd shot his own commander. One second later he himself was dead, and his comrade lay dying beside him.

The shimmering images on the hillside resolved themselves into TALON Force, running downward. Entering the cave, they found Stan kneeling beside Wu, doing his best to hold the Triad commander's femoral artery closed. Despite his efforts, bright red blood was pouring between Stan's fingers. Sarah had a tourniquet around the leg quickly, but there was no saving him.

"Wu! What are your people planning?" Travis demanded urgently.

"I will . . . not talk."

"Then you'll go to your hell with a load you'll never escape." It was all he had to work with, and it was a long shot at best. But surprisingly, it struck home. Maybe the prospect of death made Wu see his life in

a different light. It was a cinch they'd never know,
because all he could say was:

"Kauai . . . Sarin . . . two more days . . ."

And the next word came out as blood.

"Did he say 'Kauai'?" Stan asked.

"One of the Hawaiian Islands," agreed Sarah.

"That's what I heard," Jennifer said.

"I'll tell you what *I* heard," said Travis somberly.
"I heard 'two days.'"

Chapter 21

July 24, 2300 hours
Hong Kong

The bells chiming eleven p.m. from the Old First An-
glican Church were echoing softly off the towering
skyrises of Kowloon when a slight, thin guy and his
drunk date wandered into Hooker's Bar. The name
undoubtedly had a long and genteel history in the for-
mer British colony of Hong Kong, but as far back as
anybody living could remember, it was just a source
of easy jokes. And a magnet for tourists. There were
a lot of them in Hooker's tonight, and most of them
seemed as drunk as the skinny man's date. One guy,
sitting with his two investment banker friends, seemed
seriously hammered; he had to fight to hold his head
off their table. With their suitcases beside them, they
were clearly ending a wild night on the town before
leaving to catch a red-eye out of Kai Tak International. And then there was the honeymooning couple,
both good-looking, who must have made a pact not
to hit the sheets until after the clock struck twelve.
They held hands and smiled into each other's eyes,
but both kept looking at their watches.

The skinny guy wanted another drink, he told the
bartender, but his date needed the bathroom. She
started off to find it but her legs were rubbery, so
he went along to help her out. A moment later, the
honeymooners happened to follow, and then the two

bankers helped their friend to his feet. One gave the waitress a pained smile that clearly meant their friend was about to puke his guts out and they had to get him to a toilet fast.

None of them reached the bathroom.

Along the way down the narrow brown hall, the seven of them made sure they were unobserved and slipped quickly through a narrow, unmarked wooden door.

Once inside the games were over. Jennifer stopped hanging on Sam's shoulder, a position he was just starting to like. Hunter and Sarah moved as far apart as they could get. And Travis and Jack lay Stan down on an old upholstered couch. Their host, Mr. Rupert Singh, hurried to bring him a gin and tonic, on the long-held theory of tropical British colonies that quinine cured everything. He seemed disappointed when Stan waved him off, but quickly allowed the Burmese doctor he'd provided to try a more professional approach. Mr. Singh turned to the others and provided his report.

"Since you called in on your satcom unit, Major Barrett, Washington has been in an uproar. I tell you this not because I know the reason for it—which I do not—but because in all my years in service to your country I have never seen anything like it before."

"Then you'll appreciate that we're under extreme time pressures, Mr. Singh," said Travis.

"Indeed, sir." Anyone who ran a tourist bar in Hong Kong that catered to the English was hard to ruffle. "The six of you—"

"What do you mean, six?!!" demanded Stan from the couch, trying to sit up against the doctor's hands.

"Lie down, Stan, and let the doctor do his work," said Hunter.

Mr. Singh nodded at this good sense. "Lieutenant Commander Powczuk will be transferred to the medical unit of the *USS Tulsa* when she puts into port tomorrow morning—"

"The hell I will!"

"I'm afraid they warned me this would be your re-action, commander. And they told me to reaffirm that it is an order. From what Major Barrett told them, they seem greatly concerned."

"Goddamn you, Travis—"

Mr. Singh's lips tightened at the language. "Dr. Chandra, what is your opinion?"

The medical man looked up at TALON Force. "Frankly, I'm amazed the man is still alive. The bullet went completely through the pectoral muscle and the scapula. Since the caliber of the bullet was so power-ful, it broke the scapula cleanly instead of shattering it. Still, the blood loss and shock that occurred over the time since the incident happened would have killed most men. I am told . . ."—he nodded briefly toward Mr. Singh—". . . that you people have extraor-dinary medical procedures. I am also told that you've entered Hong Kong by . . . surreptitious means, which undoubtedly put an added strain on my patient. Alto-gether, I absolutely concur with the plan to ferry him to Taiwan, then fly him stateside in a hospital plane for a lengthy recuperation."

"Horse puckey!" said the reluctant patient.

Mr. Singh resumed his report. "The six of you, meanwhile, will fly to Taiwan in a small private plane for which I have arranged. There you will rendezvous with your mission transport, a V-22 Super Osprey, for a direct flight to Barking Sands Airfield at the Pacific Missile Range Facility on Kauai, one of the smaller Hawaiian islands. You must be at Kai Tak Airport within . . . one hour and ten minutes."

Chapter 22

It was a quarter past midnight when the ramshackle taxi supplied by Mr. Singh approached the airport like any other car for hire. As it neared the departures sign it took a sharp right turn and drove off the beaten track toward an area given over to international trans-shipments. A nondescript hangar, marked "29," loomed across darkened tarmac, outlined against the late glow of Kowloon City in the distance. A thin mist was beginning to lend everything a dewy sparkle.

The aircraft awaiting TALON Force Eagle Team was a Cessna Citation, standard transportation for small corporations everywhere and perfectly at home in the capitalist center of China. It could carry nine passengers in comfort and make the flight across the Formosa Strait in less than an hour. The V-22 Super Osprey would rack up another ten across the Pacific to Kauai. They would lose six hours in flying through time zones but gain back a day by crossing the International Date Line. But they had to assume that when Wu counted two days, he meant two days from a Chinese perspective, and that meant they'd have just one day left to locate the Sarin when they got to the fiftieth state.

The taxi turned inside the darkened hangar. An Oriental woman stood beside the small jet, wearing a hat

with a floppy wide brim and carrying something that
could have been a rifle under a faded raincoat. Mr.
Singh had told TALON Force to expect her, but that
didn't stop them from holding their hand weapons at
the ready.

"You recognize her?" Travis asked the driver.

"Oh yes. Very so. Mistah Singh daughtah."

Nevertheless, Travis told the man to pull up fifty
feet from the plane. He got out and approached her
on foot, his OHWS Pistol clearly visible though not
held directly on her. He looked significantly at his
watch—a new day meant a new code—and began:

"Do you have a duck?"

She replied, "I took mine to the vet."

"Was it wet?"

"No, it was after hours."

That was the correct sequence, but as always, Travis
felt like an idiot spieling such nonsense. So just for
the hell of it he added:

" 'And the end of the fight is a tombstone white,
with the name of the late deceased . . .' "

To which she replied without missing a beat:
" '. . . And the epitaph drear: "A Fool lies here, who
tried to hustle the East." ' "

She smiled and stuck out her hand. He took it and
smiled back.

"I'm Randa Singh," she said. "My father sent me
to oversee the preparations for your flight and make
certain there was no funny business."

He did not give his name in return. "Was there
any?"

"Nothing involving this hangar. A crowd of teenagers tried to do three-sixties out on the tarmac but
security chased them away. My father pays them well
to keep his occasional late-night transactions private."

"How long ago was this incident?"

"Twenty minutes. Why? Does that mean something?"

"Not to my knowledge. But the group we're up

against likes deception so I'm keeping my eyes and ears open. Everything's set here?"

She nodded. "Fully fueled under my supervision. There's food and drink."

"Okay." He called to the car, "Hunter, you're second-in-command for now. So you get to carry the suit-cases." The cases, though they appeared as if they might contain papers or files involving international banking, actually held the team's Battle Ensembles.

Hunter went around to the back and removed the suitcases from the trunk as the others exited the car. He closed the trunk and waved to the driver to thank him. The man smiled.

From the darkness of the tarmac came a sound: *Chuff!*

Before they'd consciously identified it as the bark of a rocket-propelled grenade launcher, TALON Force was diving for the ground. Travis had Randa Singh in his arm and was twisting to put himself be-tween her and the oncoming missile. But it wasn't aimed at them.

The RPG plowed into the suitcases and blew them sky high.

TALON Force was on the ground, backlit by the lurid explosion inside the hangar. They did not like being pinned down. Most of them had only OHWS Pistols and Barettas, but Jack, ever eager to have as much firepower as he could carry, was packing his XM-73 Pistol, the XM-29 Smart Rifle's little brother. Flat on his stomach he squeezed off one of the seven 15mm shells the pistol carried. It burst, spraying half a dozen 2.22mm smart bullets. From that angle on a hard flat surface, the smart bullets whined, skipped, and tumbled until anything in their trajectory might as well have been hit by a chain-link fence. The shooter had time to hear them coming, but that's all the time he had.

Kicked backward by the bullets' impact, his dead hand launched a second grenade into the midnight sky. It arced above the hangar and fell back to earth, blowing a hole in harmless marshland.

Meanwhile, Travis, Hunter, and Sarah moved as one, grabbing Randa Singh and scrambling out of the hangar, establishing a perimeter around the position where the man had fired the RPG. Jack, Sam, and Jennifer guarded the jet from any other attackers.

But there was no sign of anyone else out there. Ten minutes of sweeps turned up no other attackers. In the distant lights of the airport terminal they could see people at the huge windows craning for a look, but security stepped in to quietly and efficiently remove the gawkers. Mr. Singh had used the funds supplied by Washington to good advantage.

They regrouped and compared notes.

"My guess," said Randa, "is that the 'teenagers' dropped the man off before they fled. If so, it's my fault for not anticipating it."

"Don't blame yourself," said Travis. "As I said, the Triad is extremely crafty."

"But Randa," said Jen, "if the Triad knew we were here, they know who arranged it."

"Ohmigod!" blurted Randa, her hand shooting to her forehead in shock. "My dad—"

"And Stan!" exclaimed Hunter.

Randa pulled her Nokia cell phone from her purse. It looked like any other, but had been engineered in Arlington for secure communications when a certain code was pressed. She punched the keys with lightning speed and waited for an answer . . .

"Dad? Dad, you and your friend are in danger—"

Mr. Singh's voice came back through the ether to her ear with unruffled quietude. "You're a bit late, sweetie. But not to worry. My men dealt with it. Along with Lieutenant Commander Powczuk, over Dr. Chandra's vociferous objections. We're all fine."

Randa relayed the information to TALON, and Travis asked for the phone. "Please put the lieutenant commander on the line, Mr. Singh."

After a minute Stan said, "Uh, hello?"

"What exactly were you doing out of bed?"

"Well—"

"Never mind. From now on you obey orders and recover."

"I wouldn't *be* recovering if we'd let those guys in the office here."

Travis sighed. "Give me Mr. Singh again."

When Singh acknowledged his return, Travis said, "You realize this means your cover is blown?"

"Of course. In this business it was always just a matter of time. I will contact our masters for relocation. I know Randa would like to live in Fargo, North Dakota."

"With all due respect to Fargo—are you kiddin' me?"

"Not at all. We saw the film and cannot imagine a more exotic locale after Southeast Asia."

Well, it takes all kinds. "Sorry to be the cause of it."

"I don't consider that you are. You're fighting those who caused it, and I wish you Godspeed in blowing a hole in each of the bastards' heads."

"You're an interesting man, Mr. Singh."

"One does one's best."

Travis gave the phone back to Randa. "I wish I could detail one of my team to protect you until further arrangements have been made, but we're a man shy and running late as it is."

"Don't worry about it. I'll call two men I absolutely trust to come over and run me home."

"Then we've got a plane to catch."

July 25, 0045 hours
Formosa Strait

With Hunter at the controls over the black expanse of the Formosa Strait, TALON Force held a council of war.

"Why would that guy have shot at the suitcases," Jack was asking, "when he could have blown the jet?"

"The jet wasn't his first priority," answered Sarah. "The Ch'u Triad learned what the Battle Ensembles could do and sacrificed a pawn to destroy them."

"But I thought we killed everyone in the bunker," protested Sam.

"Did we? There could have been a dozen more guys—a hundred, even—hidden in some chamber we didn't discover. But even if we did get them all, they had time after they captured us to radio the rest of the gang, telling them their base had been infiltrated. And whatever they're doing in Kauai, or Tokyo, the commands seem to come out of Hong Kong."

"How did they know where we'd be, though?"

"We slipped into China without being detected, but once in, the most direct way out was through Kai Tak Airport. We might have exfiltrated from a clandestine air strip but they knew we couldn't spare the time. Again, they live here—they run an illegal business here. They knew the part of the airport we'd be most likely to use."

"So now we come to the big question: do they know where we're going?"

"We have to assume that they do," said Travis. "So that requires a change of plans. You know Barking Sands Airfield, don't you, Hunter?"

"I certainly do. You come in over open ocean and there are heavily wooded mountains behind the base. A prime spot for a surface-to-air missile."

"Exactly. So we're not going there directly, even though we need every minute. Once we're on the V-22, I'll change the arrangements. Even if there *are* backup ensembles available, they won't get to Kauai in time. We're going forward with no more satellite uplinks, no more invisibility. We'll have decontamination suits to protect against Sarin, but when it comes to Technologically Augmented, Low-Observable, and Networked, we've got Micro-Biochip Transmitter/Receiver implants behind our jaws and the smart weapons, and that's it. For the rest of this mission we're relying primarily on our commando training."

Rocketing through a night of massing storms, each member of the team pondered what that could mean.

Chapter 23

Lieutenant Sarah Greene stared across the Massachusetts Institute of Technology campus as brilliant lightning flashes outlined every tree and building before returning them to darkness. It was barely spring in New England, and the changing weather had brought massive thunderstorms for nearly a week. But that didn't matter to Sarah, because she had no plans to be outside, in the daytime or here in the middle of the night. She was alone, preparing for her exams in aliphatic hydrocarbons as a branch of organic chemistry, and she intended to ace them. She was, after all, working on Uncle Sam's dime.

After returning to Germany from her emergency work in Tokyo, two images were engraved in her mind. One was the ward of dying people. The other was General Krauss turning down her request to become a part of his secret operation. She had no idea what she'd missed out on, but knowing she had somehow failed drove her day and night. The general had been interested in the broad nature of her medical skills, so she set about broadening them even more. As soon as the service would transfer her to MIT, Sarah was out of Germany. She looked like a pixie, but she had a will and a pride to match anyone's.

A blast of thunder directly overhead shook the glass

in the window before her and rattled the beakers behind her. She turned to make certain her experiments hadn't been disturbed. A man was standing just outside the light from the Bunsen burner—a man she had not heard enter in the midst of rolling thunder. Smoothly, she moved toward her bag and the Baretta inside it.

As she thrust her hand into the bag, the man disappeared. Literally, vanished.

Sarah pulled the pistol and stood stock still. Another flash of lightning lit the room. There was no one else there.

But Sarah knew damn well she wasn't given to hallucinations. Someone had been in the room with her, and presumably still was. She moved to put her back against a wall, her eyes scanning the area from side to side. Standing there, another flash obliterated the shadows for a moment—and revealed a curious shimmer at the end of the bookshelves beyond the lab tables.

Sarah ran fearlessly toward the spot, and once there, swiped the area with her free hand, hitting nothing. But a soft footfall down the shadowy corridor between the shelves brought her head around. She started down the passageway, Baretta at the ready, one step at a time. It never occurred to her to call out or challenge this will-o'-the-wisp; if he was silent and invisible he wasn't there to chat. But he was there; she had no doubt.

She reached the end of the corridor and stepped boldly into the aisle, gun up. Seeing nothing, she spun into the parallel corridor—and there he was, visible and looming!

"General Krauss!" Sarah blurted in astonishment.

It was the man she'd known in Tokyo, but now he was wearing some sort of space suit. He stepped forward. "You're looking good, Lieutenant. Better than the last time we spoke."

"Thank you, sir. I am good," she replied with admirable calm. "But with all due respect—I might have shot you!"

Krauss gestured at his suit. "I'm protected."

Sarah felt her breathing tighten. "Why are you here, sir? And why are you wearing that . . . that . . . ?"

"It's called a Battle Ensemble. Top secret."

"This has something to do with your *project*?"

"Yes," Krauss answered.

"You want me to join." It was a statement. "You wouldn't show me that gear unless . . ."

"Yes."

"Thank you, sir!" Sarah all but shouted. But then, with the curiosity that drove her to a life of research, she found herself adding, "Why now, sir? Why not when we were in Tokyo?"

"In a similar situation, you would have shot me, then," said Krauss.

"Because I was near exhaustion?"

"Because you were not in control. As a doctor with your patients, yes, but as a warrior, no. First you hoped not to kill anybody, then you wanted to rid the world of a scourge. I need people who can face danger *and* face it calmly, with control. I don't need fanatics with any agenda beyond doing the job right. So I put you to a little test tonight. And you acted just as I hoped you would, showing bravery without recklessness, intelligence in the face of the unknown." He smiled his fatherly smile. "But I wouldn't have bothered if the reports on you after Tokyo hadn't continued to be so glowing."

"You kept an eye on me, even after you turned me down?"

"I have no agenda beyond doing the job right." He held out his hand. "Welcome to TALON Force."

July 25, 0115 hours
Taiwan

The turnaround in Taiwan took less than seven minutes. Mr. Singh's Cessna touched down within sight of the waiting V-22 and taxied toward it at all possible speed. When it skidded to a halt, tires smoking, TALON Eagle Team Force leapt out, scrambling for the larger transport. They had no gear to transfer, and the V-22 started rolling as soon as the cabin door was shut.

Once they were airborne, Travis went forward to work out the details of their next move. If they weren't flying straight to Barking Sands, the quickest alternative was to land at Hickam Air Force Base in Honolulu and dogleg back to Kauai on something less conspicuous. It would add maybe an hour, and time was critical, but all the time in the world wouldn't do them much good if they were shot down over the Pacific.

Meanwhile, his team took advantage of the ten-hour flight to catch some shuteye. Except for Sam. He still had the assignment of tracking down the person or persons who'd blamed the Tokyo attack on the Ya- kuza. So when Travis returned to the darkened cabin, he found Sarah, Jen, Jack, and Hunter stretched out sleeping, and one skinny guy hunched over a laptop with the look of a predator in his eyes.

"Liberia my ass!" he muttered. "The site before that one was Thunder Bay, Ontario. Still not the ori- gin point, but I'll get you, you bastard . . ."

**July 24, 1800 hours
Lihue, Kauai, Hawaii**

Kauai, on a map, looks like an old woman's head, with the profile running along the eastern coast. There on her nose is Lihue, the island's capital, about as un- Hawaiian-looking a place as you'll find; it could have been lifted out of any Midwestern state and trans- ported bodily to Nawiliwili Point. But most visitors to Kauai never see Lihue. They touch down at the air- port just outside of Lihue, meet friends or pick up their rental car, and drive off to the north side of the island, which is lush and rainy, or the south side, littered with bright and sunny coastlines.

The six "tourists" who were neither the first nor the last to leave the six p.m. Hawaiian Airlines shuttle from Honolulu might have been a little bronzer, a little buffer than most, but nothing they did drew attention to themselves. Like about a third of the passengers, they were met by a grinning native Hawaiian who hugged them all and hung leis around their necks. That proved they were tourists because leis are only given to tourists these days. And only tourists would gawk at the scenery the way these six did.

They piled themselves and their light luggage into their friend's shiny red Dodge Caravan and drove toward the south side of the island on the one major road, which ran all the way across the island until it got to the gates of the Pacific Missile Range Facility at Kauai's westernmost edge.

Along the way their old friend introduced himself.

"Fred Palauea, major, U. S. Air Force. They call me Iniki."

"Iniki? That's the hurricane that blew through in ninety-two," said Sarah. "It damaged something like seventy percent of the island!"

"Sustained wind speeds up to one hundred and forty-five miles per hour. You bet it damaged us." He gave her a wide grin. "The wind gauge on Makaha Ridge in Kokee State Park snapped off at two hundred and twenty-seven! The absolute worst thing you could possibly call somebody on Kauai is Iniki—unless you really liked 'em. It's a Hawaiian thing.

"Reason they call me Iniki is, I'm kinda like a hurricane when I get goin'. I go berserk in a fight, takin' on any bad guy I see. We're gonna be takin' on a Triad full of 'em, they tell me."

"What else did they tell you?" Travis asked.

"Just to drive over to the airport and meet six 'old friends' I'd recognize 'cause the dark-haired cutie'd have five rings in her ear. It's smart, coming in as tourists. There's thousands of you every day, so it's the best disguise you can have." He gave Sarah another grin; it seemed to be his natural expression. "What kinda commando unit lets you dress like that?"

"The only kind I'd join," she said.

"Anyway, Major," said Travis, using the man's title to end this chitchat, "down to business."

"Yes, sir. Major," answered Iniki, subtly reminding him that though Travis ran this show, they were equal in rank at the end of the day. "You flew in on Hawaiian because flying in on a V-22 might get you killed. You're here to talk a little smack with a bunch of Chinese gangbangers who got squeezed in Hong Kong and want to let the world know their feelings are hurt."

"Something like that."

"Well, you're in luck. We found the little fellas. Satellites have picked up unusual activity in a valley up the Na Pali coast. About nine miles north of where we're headed."

"Excellent, Major."

"Leave it to the Air Force," Iniki and Hunter said at once, eliciting laughs—and a few groans—in the Caravan.

"It figures they'd be on that stretch of coastline," nodded Jennifer.

"Why?" asked Sam.

Iniki answered for her. "Where you landed, at Lihue, is kinda like four o'clock on a cloak face. We're taking the southern route across the island to get to about nine. You could also take the northern road and get around to about, oh, twelve. But in between nine and twelve is the Na Pali coast, and there ain't no road there. You can't drive all the way around the island because that coastline is just one valley after another, each one separated from the other by a steep ridge coming down off Kokee Mountain. It'd be like trying to build a road across a giant's spread-out fingers, if the giant had about thirty fingers. Up an' over, up an' over, up an' over. That ain't gonna work."

"Don't the valleys flatten out as they reach the sea?" asked Hunter.

"They flatten out some, but not that much. And as they go inland, they get higher an' higher on both sides till they reach two thousand foot cliffs at the end. There's a road along the top of the cliffs, running up to Kokee State Park, but that's three or four miles inland."

"So each valley is its own private world."

"Pretty much. Of course you can fly over them and look down, but the vegetation's pretty thick. You can take a boat up the coast and look in, but as soon as the valley takes a turn you don't know what's goin' on back there."

Travis turned to Jen. "How do you know this place?"

"They film here all the time—*Jurassic Park, Indiana Jones, Six Days Seven Nights, South Pacific*."

"Yeah, I thought that was you in *South Pacific*," said Sam, apparently serious. "You're old enough to have been in the cast, aren't you?"

Jennifer whirled and punched Sam in the solar plexus, knocking him back into a howling Jack.

They were nearing Lawai and saw for the first time the extent of the cloud cover sweeping south from the peak in the middle of the island. To their left the clouds broke up and let the setting sun shine on the island's beaches, but to the right it seemed perpetually gray. Jack asked about it.

"Waialeale is the wettest spot on earth," said Iniki with local pride. "Three thousand miles of ocean evaporates moisture into the air, the trades push it in this direction, and all of a sudden it runs into a five-thousand foot peak. The almost continuous rain runs off in seven major rivers, and there's an eight-mile run of swamp up on the ridge. That's why the north shore is so lush; but the sun's here on this side, especially where we're going."

Indeed, the landscape grew brighter with each passing mile. Soon the fields grew filled with sugarcane, stark green against the rich red dirt. But that gave way in time to dryer country, and before they knew it, the Force was pulling to a halt before the gates of the Missile Facility. Iniki flashed his ID, shared a joke with the guard, and pulled around to the front of the HQ.

Standard military sod grass had been laid down around the main buildings and in the open areas between them, but these were punctuated by glorious palm trees, heavy with coconuts, and twisted, heavy-branched trees only Sarah recognized. Headquarters itself was a two-story building, the first story some twelve feet high and the second consisting mostly of a covered balcony. It looked like it would be cool on even the sunniest of days.

Beyond the usual service landscaping, the land reverted to its natural state on the driest corner of the island: sand. Beyond that lay the open Pacific, sparkling as the sun drew near its horizon. Barely visible, eighteen miles in the distance, was the small island of Niihau, the westernmost spot in the United States. Otherwise it was five thousand miles of water leading back to where they'd started this mission: Japan and China. As Hunter had said, you could see a plane coming for a long, long time.

Travis checked in with the base commander, Colonel Alvarez, a grizzled career military man who greeted him warmly, but the TALON Force commander was anxious to get moving. As soon as he could, he returned to Iniki, who was watching the sun set with the others.

"How soon can we head up to that valley?"

"We can go now if you're up for some night action."

"Of course."

"That's what I figured. I understand you're short on

your usual equipment—whatever that is—but I've got night goggles, and there'll be a full moon once it rises over Kokee. As far as weapons go—"

"That's not a problem," said Travis. "We have new pistols and rifles on our V-22, on the way across the Pacific. We brought them along on the shuttle from Honolulu, so we can supply you as well."

"That sounds like fun. I've heard a few things about you people; I'd like to get a look at what you carry."

"You got it. Now, if we can't drive up the coast, how do we get there? Fly?"

Iniki looked at him pityingly. "Why screw with the air when we've got all this water?" he said, pointing off at the Pacific. "And you're talkin' with a man who loves to fly. But I love the water more, so I'm going to give you the two-minute drill on how to paddle a Hawaiian War Canoe."

Sam looked at it doubtfully. "What if you don't love the water?" he asked.

"Two kinds'a people go up the Na Pali coast," answered the Hawaiian. "Ninety-five percent of them are tourists, in commercial boats. Could be a catamaran with a dozen folks, could be a sea kayak all by itself. If they don't camp for the night, they go right back to their bed and breakfast at the end of the day."

"How long do tourists usually camp on the beach?" asked Travis.

"Just one night, usually. But the other five percent—that's us. The native Hawaiians. And we have quite a number of *heiaus*—sacred spots—on the islands. When we go to a *heiau,* we might stay for a week. And we don't care if it's day or night when we go. So we Hawaiians are going to paddle right up to the valley, bold as brass—meaning you *haoles* and me."

"I can handle the makeup," said Jennifer.

"I knew somebody in this crew would have that covered," answered Iniki. "Let's get going on your canoe lesson."

"Not all of us," said Travis. "If these valleys are as big as you say they are, I don't want to attack from just one side. The full moon will allow Hunter and me to fly hang gliders down from those cliffs you told us about, and hit them from the rear."

Hunter grinned, a dangerous grin. "If you won't fly, Iniki, make way for those who do."

Chapter 24

Five brown-skinned, black-haired people sent their Hawaiian War Canoe skimming northward, a hundred yards off the rugged coast. There were three men and two women, the men stripped to the waist and the women wearing bright bikinis. The only odd thing, had anyone been close enough to look, was that the bikini tops looked a lot like sports bras—as if the women were planning on more than simple worship or relaxation. TALON Force was so well trained in working together that even an unfamiliar exercise like rowing this ancient craft came almost naturally to them.

"We *would* look like hell in our Battle Ensembles," muttered a sweat-slickened Sam to Sarah, "but at least they would have kept us cool."

They cut a wide angle out from the Missile Range when they put into the water, both to avoid having their departure point noticed and to avoid being spotted by the moon watchers on the public lands to the north. Soon enough the sandy, four-wheel-drive roads that skirted the Missile Range came to a halt in the dunes of Polihale State Park. Beyond, the Na Pali coast was left to only those who could travel by sea.

"Let's sing as we go!" Iniki said to Jen.

"You have got to be kidding," answered Jack.

"Not at all, Captain. Not at all. It makes the rowing easier."

"It's the rhythm method, Jack," joked Jen.

"We're just a bunch of happy Hawaiians," added Sarah, grinning at his macho discomfort. "We sing, we dance—"

"And perform Broadway showtunes!" snarled Jack. But turning from his position at the front of the canoe, he surveyed the rest of the team's faces. Seeing their looks, he sighed resignedly and started belting: "Ninety-nine bottles of beer on the wall, ninety-nine bottles of beeerrrrr . . ."

"Not exactly the Hawaiian war chant," said Iniki, "but as long as no one can hear us . . ."

And so they made their way north.

Hawaiian War Canoes sport an outrigger along the left side for stability on ocean water, while the canoers paddle on the right side. They're big boats, large enough for six or more, so it was a good thing that the boat had five physically honed warriors to propel it across the gently undulating ocean. Though tired from exertion and jet lag, the team tackled the water with enthusiasm. For days now they had been living on the edge, hurling themselves across the Pacific and back again in a race against deadly and deceptive terrorists. They were still racing, but for a moment they could paddle underneath a tropical moon and catch a little of what *most* people came to Hawaii for. There was something that excited the primitive nature in each of them—even Sam—setting out on an endless ocean in such a low-tech craft.

The moon sparkled on the blue-black Pacific, and even with all its light the sky burned with a thousand stars. Here on the ocean, the world seemed divided into two: water everywhere below, heavens everywhere above. Off to the right the bulk of Kauai loomed, but otherwise the experience was like floating in space. It was easy to see why the ancient Pacific peoples could navigate thousands of miles from one tiny island to another; once you learned the stars you could never get lost. And even now, an hour after sunset, it was still warm. Not warm enough to sit on the shore without a wrap, perhaps, but just right for the exercise of rowing along the calm water.

It's easy to forget, when standing on an island, that once the water starts it doesn't stop for a long, long way. In a boat, however, any distance at all off the shore shows the island for what it is: a small piece of ancient volcano top sticking out of a vast expanse of briny blue. Kauai is only thirty-three miles east to west, and twenty-five north to south.

From their canoe, TALON Force could see the wide sand beaches sweeping up to jumbled rocks at the beginnings of the canyons. The canyons then swept up into the tangled darkness of the lush jungle. The first mountain peaks lay behind, the high peak of the volcano beyond permanently wrapped in clouds. It was hard to believe, as the warm ocean breezes swept over them, that it was always raining within easy view.

Travis had had no doubt that those cliffs would have turned some of the airmen at the Missile Range Facility into hang-gliding enthusiasts. All he had to do was ask and he and Hunter were supplied with two beautiful gliders to take up top.

The two men piled them in the back of Iniki's van and drove off the base. Five miles down the line, at the village of Kekaha, they turned left onto the Kokee Road. As they left the flatlands along the beaches the island spread out below and around them like a beautiful quilt. Soon, however, the land to their right began to fold in upon itself, changing from tree-covered hills to plummeting gorges. As they drove, the van hugged the rim.

Since they were moving inland, closer to the peaks, the moon now sliding over the eastern heights, flooding the world with light and revealing Waimea Canyon on their right. Mark Twain called Waimea "the Grand

Canyon of the Pacific"; though not nearly as big, it had the same sculpted walls laced with multicolored layers of minerals, all descending from what once was an expansive mesa. Hang-gliding into all that beauty, by moonlight, would have been an experience of a lifetime. Unfortunately, Travis and Hunter would be flying from the other side of the ridge road, and they weren't thinking much about the beauty of their surroundings. Their minds were on the kill.

Some fourteen miles from the turnoff, they came to the side road Iniki had shown them on their map. It was paved for about a mile before a second road turned off of it. This was a dirt road cutting deep into the high-elevation forest. They were close to four thousand feet here, but the gradual slope of the land toward the sea would bring them back to two thousand or so before they reached the point they'd picked, high above the valley where the mysterious activity had been reported.

An hour and a half after leaving the Missile Range, the red van rolled to a halt at a dusty pull-off. Travis and Hunter got out and set to work. First they used shielded flashlights to make their way out a narrow but serviceable path to the cliff edge. They had to make certain no amorous couple was lying on a blanket, enjoying the view, something Iniki had warned them was a distinct possibility. Fortunately, the amorous couples had gone elsewhere tonight. They were alone.

The next step was to make sure they stayed that way. They returned to the van and removed the gliders from the back, then took a couple of pairs of underpants, which had been donated to the cause, and hung them rakishly on the doors, which they left wide open. A kerosene lamp inside the van would make the underwear visible to anyone driving into the pull-off, and it would take an especially amorous couple not to decide to find a place with more privacy, not to mention more class.

Then they carted the gliders back out along the path and set about assembling them. Ahead of them was a two thousand foot drop to the back of the valley, which lay in deep shadows and would stay that way until the moon got an hour higher. From all that darkness came the soft and distant bleating of wild goats, and above lay the silence of stars.

Chapter 25

Two hours after the War Canoe pushed off from the Missile Facility, the Na Pali coastline changed into one far different from the dry, sandy beaches the five-person crew had left. The closer the rowers got to the rainy side of the island, the greener and wilder—and cooler— it got. Each canyon they passed seemed steeper and narrower than the last, more thickly choked with trees and fallen boulders. Clearly, nature was pretty much doing what it wanted to do up here.

Abruptly, Iniki held up a hand, halting their rendition of "New York, New York."

"We're getting close," he said, careful not to point. Just as the island became perfectly visible beneath the high-riding moon, so were they if anyone was watching from shore. "Around that next ridge."

They redoubled their efforts, and the canoe responded by surging forward like a hog at feeding time. They slid past the ridge, a gigantic ripple in the earth, and a valley opened up before them—a valley no different from the last three, as far as the TALON Force members could tell. There was a narrow beach guarded by half-submerged boulders, against which the sea was crashing with huge spumes of whitewater. On the beach, above the high-water mark, a second jumble of boulders showed where centuries of fallen rock had ended up.

A river sparkled inland as it made its way to the sea, then surged through a cut in the rocks. Beyond, there was nothing but the black-green jungle sweeping up and away to the gray cloud-covered peaks a good distance behind.

"That's going to be a tricky deal, getting in there," Sam offered, eyeing the offshore rocks.

"That's why I'm going to put you up on the prow, Sam," answered Iniki. "To spot the rocks and push us off as we go by."

"What?!"

He was answered by chuckles up and down the boat. He turned and tried to glare, but soon had to smile himself. He knew who had the muscles on the team to paddle forcibly away from obstacles, and it wasn't him.

"Well, how was I to know?" he asked them. "Who knows what crazy shit these Hawaiians get up to? Running rapids in the moonlight! How nuts is that?"

"Be that as it may," said Iniki, "we're running those rocks right now, relying on my impeccable skill and you guys' strong right arms. Ready?"

"No," said Sam.

"Good. Now, I want you all to paddle on my count. But when I say stop, stop. When I say go, go. We can do this if we stay right on top of things."

"It's being on top of those rocks that I'm—"

"*One*-two. *One*-two. *One*-two." Iniki overrode him. Sam steeled himself for the task, as prepared as anyone to do his share; what he lacked in muscle he made up for in determination.

On Iniki's count, the war canoe turned toward the beach and quickly picked up speed as the waves caught it from behind. As they swept toward the rocks, the way through was not at all apparent, but Iniki's chant was full of good cheer. All at once the water dropped out from under them as they found themselves on the crest of a breaking wave.

"Faster!" cried Iniki. "*One*-two-*one*-two-*one*-two-*one*-two—"

Paddling furiously, the canoe barreled forward like a rocket. The wave crashed beneath them and the first rocks appeared dead ahead.

"Left! Left, dammit!" Sam shouted.

The canoe was wonderfully responsive but it seemed there'd be no time to turn it enough before they impacted the rocks. As it was, they scraped their right side as they surged past. A wave crashing to their left blinded them. "Faster!" Iniki bellowed.

Now there was a scraping sound from below. Iniki was taking them *over* a rock, riding the swell. They were just a fraction late—the water ran out from under them and they balanced for a moment on barnacle-encrusted stone before sliding forward into a pool. Then a new wave struck them from behind and rocketed them sideways toward another boulder. "Stop!"

They stopped. The wave continued to carry them, but as its force ran out they had time to turn the boat toward a narrow opening before the next wave took them. They surged toward it. "Right!" Sam directed.

They paddled toward the opening between the jagged rocks. Water forced into the cleft between the boulders shot them out the other side with their outrigger riding up on the rock, tilting the canoe at a 45 degree angle. But they were still heading forward. "Go!" Iniki shouted as the canoe dropped back to the horizontal and continued onward.

Now they were past the worst of it. The rocks were smaller but still there, and some of them were completely submerged, hard to see in the gray light of the moon. If they hadn't had Iniki they'd have been hard put to make it all the way, and they certainly would have totaled the canoe. But they avoided the lurking dangers and rode at last to a scrunching halt on the silvery sand.

The big man leapt out and grabbed the prow, starting to pull the craft up out of the water. Iniki called to them with boisterous humor, in Hawaiian. They didn't need to be told that *they* were Hawaiian for the purposes of this exercise, and almost as one, they jumped from the canoe themselves and helped him get it up to a safe location.

Cheerfully talking a blue streak, the big man led them up the sandy slope toward a weatherbeaten but well-maintained hut. Outside the building were various offerings to the polyglot gods of the island—flowers, liquor bottles, plastic statues of Mary, bananas. They went inside, and once they were hidden by the building's walls they knew exactly what to do. As Iniki began a rambling discourse on the souls of their ancestors and the wonderful festivities they'd be running through to pay homage to said souls, Jen, Jack, Sarah, and Sam took out six-cell flashlights from the colorful cloth bags they carried. Lighting a kerosene lamp primarily to mask the flashlight beams, they started searching for listening devices.

It didn't take long for their trained eyes to find some.

Jennifer signaled the others over to a crack between the hut's planks. Where other cracks were just cracks, this one was filled in with something that turned out to be plastic, made to look like wood. Digging in the plastic would only create suspicious sounds so they kept it in mind as they kept looking. Soon Jack found a second spot like the first, on the other side of the hut.

When they were certain there was nothing else— especially cameras—Sam removed a scanner from the large bag Jenny carried. He set it in the center of the hut and began to slowly sweep 360 degrees. After three minutes, he returned the scanner to two positions it had passed over and showed the others the blips on the screen: two more listening devices, most likely small parabolic microphones like the ones seen on the sidelines of National Football League games.

They were set at each end of the beach, no doubt camouflaged among the palms and boulders.

All in all, this beach was wired for sound. The Triad was taking no chances.

Now that they knew where the danger points lay, it was time to move inland, for the religious ceremony they were supposed to be having. Again, Iniki kept up a cheerful chatter—since nobody else could—as the "Hawaiians" went back to their canoe and unloaded bags with food and drink sticking out of the tops. If the bags clanked a little when set down on the sand, not even the most paranoid listener at the mikes' receiving station could make much out of it. As they stood among the breaking waves, far from the mikes and covered by the sound of the surf, the team added up what it knew.

The Ch'u Triad had a base back in this jungle. Because they were on public (if infrequently visited) land, their defensive devices had to be less obtrusive than the ones they used in their bunker. They would know when people came to visit, but they probably wouldn't know who they were. With something big scheduled for tomorrow, they would have to send a patrol toward the beach to see what was up. So TALON Force had to get off the beach and disappear into the jungle as soon as possible.

As the moon reached its highest point in the overarching sky, the group crossed the sand and took a trail leading into the valley with Iniki in the lead. Within moments, the sound of the surf behind them was swallowed up, replaced by the night sounds of the tropical jungle.

They donned their standard-issue night goggles. After the thermal sensing of the Battle Ensemble, the goggles seemed clumsy and dim. But once the moonlight was blotted out by the overhanging trees, they couldn't have gone ten feet without them. And they really didn't mind much operating in tropical clothing instead of the suits' bulk.

They also took their new XM-29 Smart Rifles from the colorful bags and carried them at the ready. Their XM-73 pistols and Barettas went in shoulder holsters, along with extra ammo carts. Iniki had been issued his own set of TALON Force weapons for this mission. They were betting that the Triad was far enough back in the valley that a patrol would take some time in reaching them, but it wasn't a bet they were willing to back with their lives. It was unlikely that the Triad would slaughter what was supposed to be a bunch of innocent Hawaiians; the island was too small, tourism was too important, and the natives were too communal. More likely the intruders would simply be rounded up at gunpoint to be held until tomorrow's deadline had passed. But once the Triad saw who the intruders were, anything was possible.

Finally, they took rucksacks packed with the rest of their supplies from the bags and ditched the bags in foliage well off the trail. Now they were ready for the hunt.

Chapter 26

After a fresh scan by Sam failed to unearth any listening devices within range, they took the opportunity of contacting Travis and Hunter high on the cliffs above. Because the Micro-Biochip Transmitter/Receiver was an implant, it functioned in a limited fashion without the rest of the Battle Ensemble. On its own it could communicate with other members of TALON Force using line-of-sight transmission for up to a thousand meters; this would come in handy on this hike. But Travis and Hunter were on the very edge of that range, if they were in it at all, and line-of-sight was out of the question while the five were under the canopy of trees. Sam had to use a handheld transceiver.

"What do you see from up there?" Sam asked.

"Not a damn thing. This high up, it's just a carpet of darkness down to the sea. We'll need you guys to pinpoint an area for us when the time comes," answered Travis.

"And you really plan to jump off a two thousand foot ridge under those conditions."

"Beats stumblin' around in the mud. You just say the word and we'll be down."

"Down thousands of feet right into the jungle. That's what I'm worried about."

"Since when did you become my nagging mother?"

answered Travis, keeping his troops loose. "Just make sure to give us an accurate location while you're stumbling around down there in the dark."

The five on the ground were certainly doing its share of stumbling. It was a muddy trail, as most trails on Kauai are; the red dirt held a lot of rain and was extremely slippery. Slipping off the narrow trail was no picnic, since it tended to run along the edge of the bank overlooking the river. The steep bank was covered with vegetation, so there was no telling what was hidden there. A rock, a tree root, a hole—perhaps even dangerous animals.

There were no overt signs of previous hikers. But there were signs of previous hikers' prints being covered by the dragging of leaves, if one knew how to look for them. Which TALON Force did.

As soon as he could, Iniki lifted a hand, spread his fingers, then rolled it over with fingers cocked like a gun, pointing toward a vague path running upward between two groves of trees.

The path had been used before, but not recently. Jack drifted forward to Iniki. "This go somewhere?" he murmured. Iniki had no Micro-Biochip implant, but Jack had long since mastered the art of speaking so that no one but the person next to him could hear.

"Up the hillside. Steep. Tough going in some spots but it won't be used by the Triad," Iniki whispered back.

The track grew less distinct as it rose. After a quarter of an hour they took another, moving onward parallel to the original path but five hundred feet higher up. The new path was extremely vague, and the team followed Iniki's surefooted steps through the thick overgrowth. It was TALON Force's practice to cultivate local contacts during their missions, and Iniki was proving to be a good one. But then, reflected Jennifer, Randa Singh and her father had been topflight, too. She wasn't so certain she could say the same about Yuki Kurimoto. He'd been efficient, but there'd been no rapport. Not that you needed rapport to do your job, but she hadn't realized until then how much Kurimoto had gotten on her nerves. Maybe it was the contrast with Iniki, who treated her as a female capable of performing every bit as well as a man, unlike the stoic Japanese. Maybe it was just that Kurimoto was a jerk.

They went onward in silence.

In his own mind, Jack was getting primed for the payoff, looking forward to tackling this unfamiliar jungle and wiping out another nest of Triad goons. And all they had as far as high-tech weaponry were the anti-Sarin protective suits and the knowledge of how to decontaminate if attacked. And firepower. Sarin was a weapon of mass destruction, best used in enclosed spaces, so Jack thought it unlikely that the Triad would use it against them out here in the open jungle. But the best way to be sure the Sarin wouldn't be unleashed was to kill the gangbangers first. Jack revered Sun Tzu and his *The Art of War*, but he also had a soft spot for the Spaniard Dominic Guzmán, who sometime after founding the Dominican Order of the Catholic Church went to war with the cry, "Kill them all! God will recognize His own!"

Sam had one eye on his scanner and one eye on the nonexistent trail. It was his job to do the things the other members of TALON Force couldn't, such as handling the electronics end of things. And in the twenty-first century, that end was only getting bigger and bigger. But it also distinguished him from the others, as well. That, and his skinny body.

They'd been walking for almost an hour when Sam muttered one word: "Down." The TALON Force members heard him through the Micro-Biochip Transmitter/Receiver and dropped in unison. Iniki followed their reaction and scuttled crabwise with them into the vegetation as far as they could go without undue noise.

Then they heard what Sam's scanner had picked up: people moving along a cross path. Soon three Chinese came into view, fifteen feet ahead, talking quietly amongst themselves. They held their AK-47s at the ready, taking occasional looks around. They were on patrol, but not a very rigorous one. They obviously had no idea anyone was nearby.

Thirty feet farther on, the patrol's radio crackled into life. One of them, obviously the leader, had a short conversation. His voice was not loud but it carried clearly enough on the still night air. Then the patrol moved onward, with somewhat more urgency.

"Their commander is getting pretty worried about us," said Sam. "Evidently they still lean toward the idea that we're just here for a luau and some old time religion, but they can't figure out where we went. Maybe we're at some hidden temple offering up a sacrificed pig. So they're calling on patrols off our expected path to help spot us."

"Let's pick up the pace, Iniki," answered Jack. "Get on 'em while they're still wondering."

TALON Force moved out with even more urgency, and in another twenty minutes they were over two ridges and at the top of a third. They were about to keep going when Sam halted them, staring at his scanner. He turned to stare below.

"Communication central down there," he said, then used his radio to contact Travis. "Boss, we've got 'em spotted. You locked on my signal?"

"I could flick a fly off your ear."

"Hold that thought. Look off maybe seven hundred meters to the north-northeast."

"Okay. There's nothing visible from up here, but I see a likely landing spot. Just a break in the trees, but we can do it. You say 'when.' "

"All right. We'll recon down this slope. Stay alert."

"Damn, Sam. And here I was just about to turn in for the night."

The Force made its way carefully down the hillside, Sam continuously alert for any electronics locking in on their position. They were making a wide detour halfway along when he spotted another listening device thirty meters ahead. After adjusting their route, they were soon working their way into the flatlands.

It wasn't long after that they heard voices, from what appeared to be a clearing near the river—no more than fifty feet ahead. Iniki motioned a halt so Sam could listen in again. When he was done he motioned Iniki to get close while he gave the others the highlights.

"Nobody's found us and they don't like it. They're going to add two patrols to the one already out there and sweep toward the coast, one along the river and one on either side."

"Good," gritted Jack. "We'll give them twenty minutes to get away from our position, then take what's left."

It was a good plan but it couldn't account for the call of nature to those who stayed in the Triad's camp. After ten minutes a man carrying a roll of toilet paper popped out of the trees and stared them straight in the eyes. He jumped backward as if he were strung on a bungee cord, shouting out in Chinese. Sam gave his own bark.

"Travis!"

"Yo!"

"Now!"

The ground team was already scrambling forward, weapons up at their shoulders. They burst upon the clearing and threw themselves behind the last rocks and trees, firing with honed precision. Five of the Chinese went down almost at once, taken out by the XM-29s' smart bullets, but fifteen others had the chance to find their own cover and return fire.

"Ten minutes isn't enough for the patrols to get out of earshot!" snapped Jack. "They'll be back in five, so do what you have to do!"

Sam was snapping off single shots, picking his targets with care. This was something he had a real aptitude for, after all those years of video games. Iniki took out two of the men beside a prefab cabin the Chinese had erected, opening up that side of the clearing. Then suddenly, with the force and speed of his hurricane namesake, he jumped up, darted for the cabin's corner, and opened up another angle of fire, spraying the entire clearing with a round of fire. As he neared the cabin a face appeared momentarily at a window. Iniki threw himself flat as a hail of bullets tore a hole in the cabin's plastic side and sang over his head. He waited until the burst blew itself out, then rolled to his side and returned the fire. A cry from inside the hole was cut off by lead, becoming a wrenching gurgle.

Sam jumped and ran ten yards to his left, then ten more, as he set up a third angle of attack. Now the defenders' shelter was severely reduced and caught in a crossfire. The other TALON Force members rolled and ran to positions between Sam and Iniki, forming a crude semicircle. But the Chinese had learned their trade in a rough part of the world and knew their business as well. They also knew who they had to be facing, and what these people had done to their friends in the bunker. Several of them raked the area with strafing fire as others broke for the far side of the clearing. Half of them didn't make it, but the rest disappeared into the thick green.

"Jen!" said Jack. "They'll try to circle back on us. Guard our right flank and I'll take the left."

"On my way."

The Saks saleswoman would *really* have goggled at her customer now. Jen's beauty was never more apparent or less important as her lithe figure slipped through the Hawaiian foliage. She hadn't gone more than fifty meters from the clearing before she encountered the Triads who had tried to circle around them. Her weapon rode easily in her hands as her bullets tore a hole through the greenery, leaving it spouting red.

She bent low and ran on past the downed men,

looking for more. A curious whisper reached her ears as she went by them.

"But . . ." gasped one of the Chinese, his eyes wide as if seeing her and all of infinity, ". . . but you're a woman . . ."

"Damn straight, cowboy. I am woman, hear me blow you to hell," she answered, ending the man's sputtering with a quick double-tap of her Baretta.

Jack had the side closest to the ocean, the direction in which the two patrols had gone. He didn't encounter anyone trying to outflank them—had they all gone Jen's way?—but he did hear the sounds of the patrols crashing back as fast as they could. He spun and hurled himself behind a fallen tree trunk, resting his weapon on the moss-covered surface. As they appeared out of the jungle he picked off two before they knew what hit them.

The others threw themselves behind the trees and set up a ring of fire, which they gradually attempted to widen just as TALON Force had done back at the clearing. It was an interesting setup, Jack thought. These guys in front of me and the main fight behind me. If any of the Chinese takes it into his head to slip up behind me, I'm dead meat. But my team knows what's going on over here, so they'll cover me. He never doubted it for an instant.

The problem was, the Triads in front of him were trying to stage their own flanking actions, struggling to get back to the main firefight. One man couldn't hold them all at bay. When bullets started flying from both Jack's right and his left, it was time to think about protecting his team's backside. The guys on his left would come out behind TALON Force if he gave them half a chance. So turning to the right, Jack pumped off two 20mm grenades from the bottom barrel of the XM-29, then swiveled to his left to fire at the flankers. The grenades, with electronic fuses that burst automatically when in range, turned the jungle to his right to splinters.

Jack was in the midst of alerting the Force through the Micro-Biochip Transmitter about the flankers to his left when a shout of Chinese erupted from the clearing. He didn't need to know the words to know what it said. He only had to know that what goes up must come down.

Soaring from the pre-dawn sky were Travis and Hunter on their ultralites, firing nonstop at the attackers below them like avenging angels. The Triads frantically burrowed their way into makeshift shelters, but they proved to be no defense against a skyborne attack.

The survivors turned their weapons to the heavens, but that brought renewed firing from the ground forces. TALON Force wasn't going to let its most exposed members take any flak. And Travis and Hunter, faded silhouettes against the fading stars, were old hands at this sort of warfare, slipping and sliding through the air with bewildering speed. Bullets tore the sky where their muzzle flashes had been, but the gliders were long gone. Then a shooter would catch one from Sam or Sarah or Jen or Iniki, one less worry for the flyboys.

The remaining defenders couldn't take it any more. They broke and ran. But even as they did a new sound rode the jungle breeze. A low, thundering roar from maybe half a mile away. And not *one* roar. Almost like—

"Planes!" Hunter yelled.

Rising in the gray sky was a DC-10. An airliner!

"How the hell can that take off from a jungle?" Sarah demanded of no one in particular.

"I dunno," answered Sam, "but they're doing it again!"

Indeed, a second DC-10 followed the first into the inky skies.

Chapter 27

If the Chinese had felt like grouping together for a last stand along the trail leading from the clearing toward the planes, they might have done themselves some good. But they were thoroughly separated from each other now, running as fast as they could into the distance. So it was that TALON Force came over a rise into another, deeper canyon—and witnessed a bizarre sight.

Stretching from one side of the canyon to the other was a vast web of camouflage netting—over half a mile from side to side and covered with leaves and chopped foliage to make it invisible from the air. The valley floor had been smoothed as if by earth movers, providing for an asphalt runway—indeed, the smell of the warm blacktop hit them for the first time on the tropical air. Along the runway, portable lights were blazing, lighting up the path and the netting above it.

The amount of work that had been put into this base was staggering, especially when you realized it had to be kept secret. Given that the Na Pali coast was rarely visited, and any particular valley even less so, there would still have to be a significant amount of sea traffic involved in smuggling the earth-moving equipment. And then, bringing in two airliners . . . Hunter, touching down in his glider from the rear, could see it in his mind's eye: the planes would have made late-night runs, just above the waves, hugging the treetops before landing. The landing lights would be flashed as little and as quickly as possible, so it would take master pilots and a highly trained ground crew to make a successful landing. The sound of the motors would attract attention, but anyone who heard it—almost certainly Hawaiians visiting *heiaus*—could be forgiven for assuming the planes were headed for the Air Force base down the coast. Once the planes got among the mountains, the sound would echo and reflect; it would be tough to decide where it was coming from.

But it could be done. Hell, it had been done. And all of a sudden, the Triad's whole plan unfolded inside Hunter's head as if he'd designed it himself. Commercial aircraft could penetrate civilian areas that military aircraft would be stopped long before reaching. Commercial aircraft could fly right over Tokyo—or the other way, to California . . .

Carrying Sarin.

Hunter burst past the others, running headlong—even tripping and sprawling headlong, only to roll back onto his feet in one motion. His voice crackled in the others' ears: "There's an F-4 still parked down there!" The others ran after him.

Once he reached the flattened soil at the canyon's base he ran at an angle toward the obsolete American jet. Gunfire stitched the ground beside him, but before it could correct itself it was cut off by the accurate, deadly fire from the team behind him. Now he spotted a lone Chinese also running toward the jet. It was a foot race, and Hunter had already run a good distance. He forced the pain in his lungs and legs aside and increased his speed.

The Chinese decided to stop running long enough to turn and fire at him. It was a bad move all around. The guy was breathing heavily from his exertions so he didn't have a hope in hell of aiming well, and it gave the rest of TALON Force a chance to take their own shots. It also gave Hunter the time to make up some distance. However, TALON Force's shots were no more on target than the Chinese soldier's, so he went back to running unscathed. But now the race was a dead heat.

One hundred meters. Fifty meters. Twenty. Slowly but surely the Chinese was gaining the advantage as their two tracks converged. Now the man was at the jet, scrambling up the side into the cockpit. His gloved hands stabbed at the controls.

But Hunter vaulted into the space and landed hard against the ladder's rungs. The Chinese would have to deal with him before he could take control of the jet. The man had the leverage of the pilot's seat and used it to thrust upward, trying to dislodge Hunter, who was now wedged between the cockpit and the canopy. But Hunter was ready for that and scrapping for anything he could hold onto.

The Chinese used one hand to hold him off and with the other pulled back on the throttle. The jet began to move down the runway, unsteady but picking up speed. It was not the wisest move on the pilot's part; if he didn't get Hunter loose in time he'd be trying to take off with the cockpit still open. Then they'd both be screwed.

Other members of the Triad, somewhere in the jungle, started firing at Hunter's legs, trying to help their comrade. Again, the wavering progress of the jet defeated that maneuver; and almost immediately cooler heads prevailed. If they put enough holes in the plane it wouldn't matter who won the wrestling match.

Hunter took his eyes off his opponent long enough to see where they were on the runway. In just seconds they'd either have to go up or roll off the asphalt. It had to be ended now!

Hand to hand, both men twisted—Hunter sideways, the Chinese backward. It gave Hunter a moment's opening—he swung a fist down and shattered the Triad's nose with the meaty part of his palm, driving the splintered bone into the man's brain. The Triad's body went limp immediately, and Hunter used all of his strength to haul his body out of the cockpit, letting it fall to the tarmac below. It hit the asphalt with the sound of a coconut shattering, the legs and arms sprawling in all directions.

The jet's forward progress slowed, rolling uncertainly to a halt. Hunter, unwilling to risk a renewed round of gunfire, rolled into the cockpit.

Ahead, the second DC-10 was just now disappearing into the red-gray light of dawn.

Hunter was already drawing the helmet and goggles left behind by his adversary over his eyes. He wheeled the jet in a tight circle and headed back the way they'd come. There was no other way to get airborne; the amount of runway left in the direction of takeoff was too limited for him. Everything depended on the Triad not knowing who was at the controls. As he passed the spot where the Triad fire had come from he turned, grinned, raised his thumb. The landing lights threw light from below, so a man in the cockpit was in shadow. The landing lights half-blinded the men on the ground, who hadn't reached the body yet.

He got back to his starting point and spun the jet around again. Now the time for pretense was done.

"I'm going after those planes," he rasped into his Micro-Biochip Transmitter.

"Kick one down for me," snapped Travis in his ear.

"And the other for me!" yelled Jen.

Hunter revved the jet engines, building momentum. Everyone on the ground pulled back from the runway as the sound built to a scream—then he yanked the throttle and started forward. The little jet was nimble, maybe too nimble for the makeshift tarmac, but Hunter held it together and before he knew it he was airborne and gone.

The other members of TALON Force Eagle Team watched Hunter rocket away into the blue—then a sixth sense honed by too many missions set off an alarm in Jack's head. "Down!" he screamed, just as he caught troop movement from the corner of his eyes.

They had no sooner hit the red dirt than bullets started whistling overhead. They rolled for cover at the base of the slope and fired back. Pinned down, Sam got on the horn.

"PMRF, this is Luau-1. We have two aircraft that need attention. PMRF, can you read me?"

The receiver returned nothing but a shrieking hiss. Sam spun the dial, trying another frequency, then another.

"I'm not getting any response, Travis."

"Too far down in these valleys?"

"I wouldn't think so. It could be some geologic formation blocking the signal."

"Or a Triad jamming device."

"Right about now I'm missing our Battle Ensemble satellite uplink."

"Travis?" Sarah's voice piped in.

"Yeah, Sarah?"

"Is it me or do these guys not seem as crazy about fighting us as they did ten minutes ago?"

"I was thinking they were lacking a little intensity."

Sam's voice answered: "They're just trying to hold us in place. Now that the planes are airborne . . ."

Travis said, "We need to turn the page, people. On my command, flank 'em and finish 'em. But not permanently, if you can avoid it. I want Sam to talk to these guys."

It was over within fifteen minutes. The Chinese had lost their fighting drive with the departure of the planes, but they weren't into losing their lives. Their counterparts in the bunker back in China had fought a lot harder, but then, they were defending their home base—and they had no other option since they were all underground together. When the deadly fire from TALON Force's XM-29s offered these guys capture or death, they chose capture. Soon six of them were lined up along the runway.

"Who's your top man?" Sam demanded, and the group threw sideways glances toward a man nearly as wide as he was tall, whose pockmarked skin was set off by a jagged knife scar.

"What are the planes' destination?"

"I don't know. And if I did I wouldn't tell you."

"You know Mr. Wu?"

Warily the man responded, "Maybe."

"He tried to stall for time and took a bullet."

The man laughed. Then, when he saw that Sam's face was completely serious, he drifted to an uneasy halt.

"You're going to tell us everything you know."

"It won't do you any good. The Triad has blocked all transmissions off this little island."

Sam gave him a very hard glance. "Sarah, try the radio again."

"Still nothing, Sam."

Sam turned back to the gang leader. "You can't stop telephone and satellite transmissions."

The assumption gave the man back his bravado. "You don't know what you're up against."

"That's right. But you're going to enlighten us." He looked at the others in his team and explained what the man had said.

"Whatever we learn," said Travis instantly, "it won't do us any good if we can't communicate it. We're heading back to your canoe and then the Missile Facility as fast as we can make it. I'll talk to this bastard in the canoe."

"Wait!" It was Jen. "Hunter's not on the island! He's not subject to their jamming while he's in the air!"

Sam turned back to the Triad member. "You forgot about the jet."

"Pfagh! The jet was prepared for the possibility of its falling into unfriendly hands. It has no radio."

Sam turned to Travis. "Let's go!"

Chapter 28

As Hunter Blake banked his F-4 into the clear Pacific sky, he could see the two passenger planes off to the east, black beads against the rising sun. He switched on the VHF radio and punched up Guard Channel, the international emergency frequency, to alert the Missile Range Facility, and through them the Air Force High Command . . . but got no response. Not even static. He ran the dial up and down but was met with only silence.

The radio was disabled.

He thought it through, as he automatically brought the jet into line behind the other craft. The Chinese's use of the Nam-era jet was a smart move. As an American plane, it wouldn't excite much attention. As an obsolete American plane, it wouldn't immediately signal a threat. Hell, the Triad expected to use it themselves. But they knew they were in a clandestine situation on an unfriendly island, in an area they couldn't completely secure, just up the coast from an Air Force facility. They were prepared for disaster and had rigged the jet to contain it. Anyone using this plane to catch their airliners would be cut off from the outside world, unable to sound an alarm. Well, that was all right; the rest of TALON Force would handle that,

Hunter thought. But as he followed the airliners toward a cruising altitude of thirty thousand feet, Hunter had to wonder what else they might have rigged to contain the damage. Was there even now some timing device clicking down toward cancellation of this unauthorized flight?

If so, there wasn't a goddamn thing he could do about it, so he put it out of his mind.

What day was it? Friday? Yes, it was. Four days since Tuesday at the Ministry of Finance in Tokyo, but they'd gained back a day crossing the date line. The airliners had a five and a half hour flight at DC-10 speeds, and would lose three more time zones before they reached the California coast in the middle of the afternoon. Most people would still be in their offices . . . the cities would be full . . .

Below and to his right was the island of Oahu. He considered putting down at Dillingham or Hickam, but flying any kind of jet into a Naval air station with no radio contact would be dangerous at best. On the other hand, he should have shown up on their radar by now, and they could be scrambling to come greet him. Only they weren't. So at worst, or best, they'd be radioing him to see what was up and getting no response. If it was a slow day, they might send somebody up to check him out, but it would have to be a damn slow day, with him flying away from the islands already. More likely, they'd put him on report for when he came in for a landing someplace else.

Because if they were looking at anything on their screens now, it would be the two airliners.

Okay. Say the Triad paid an air traffic controller to log them in as normal scheduled flights—somehow keeping them from raising a red flag as they passed across Hawaiian air space. TALON Force should still have sounded its own alert by now. But there was nothing. Could TALON Force have been trapped at the base? Killed? It didn't seem very likely. The Force was mortal—the Force could die, but not against that meager opposition. As nasty as the Triad was, they preferred to gas innocents from hiding; they hadn't shown the stomach to shoot it out with TALON Force and win. But what was the alternative? That TALON Force's radio had been shut down, too?

Well, it was a cinch that Hunter wasn't going to find out the answer any time soon. And if no one was going to come help him, he was going to have to operate off his own instincts. Which at the moment found him shadowing the DC-10 farthest to the north because it took him farthest away from the islands. Far to the south he could see Maui and the Big Island. The other plane was already diverging into another flight path away from his position.

Hunter increased his speed and moved up on the larger craft. Now that the light was coming up in the east, he could see the plane more clearly, and he didn't like what he saw. For one thing, there was metal sheathing the plane's markings on its top and sides, and more around its tail—as if the damn plane were wearing a disguise. And for another thing, it had been outfitted with 2.75-inch rocket pods and what looked like 50-caliber heavy machine guns!

Hunter squeezed the trigger on his own guns, to see if they'd been disabled like his radio, and was very glad to find that they hadn't. He had a chance to bring these planes down, a very good chance so long as he stayed beside or behind them, where their forward-mounted armament couldn't touch him. They had him outgunned, but no DC-10 could even begin to participate in a dogfight. Even if the plane to the south turned to help its companion, it was too far away and too sluggish to get over in the time it would take Hunter to down the first one.

He squeezed off another burst past the windscreen of the DC-10, to announce to "Flight Triad" that their sightseeing was done. Then he moved up parallel to it, off its left wing. He wanted a look at the crew's faces. He was close enough to read their expressions, and they weren't the looks of a bewildered airline crew. The men in that cockpit were clearly looking at an enemy. They waggled their wings at him to announce their peaceful intentions; he paid no attention to that.

He pointed down, signaling them to land.

They stared. They conferred. Then, with the same hateful expressions but all-too-stagy shrugged shoulders, they turned the craft away from him, into a wide turn, exposing the plane's wide underbelly.

In that underbelly, the baggage hold door exploded open.

From that hold a man strapped in a web of netting opened fire with a mounted .50-caliber gun.

Hunter hadn't expected that. The bullets rocketed across the intervening space and rattled off the F-4's fuselage. Instantly, that fuselage was gone, as Hunter was forced to take evasive maneuvers. Two seconds later he was four hundred feet above the DC-10 and the man in the baggage compartment couldn't get at him.

That was all right with Hunter. He was doing his own shooting now, and the big passenger jet was an easy target. His finger was wrapped around the control-stick trigger and the pounding of the high-velocity 30mm revolver cannon surged through his body. The AP-tipped shells surged through the skies and stitched the airliner's huge tail. If it was loaded with Sarin, as he suspected, there was no better place to send it than into the ocean, now hundreds of miles from land.

But at the same moment, Hunter felt far more than the muffled recoil of his own guns. He felt the slamming impact of shells in his right wing. Instantly he compensated, sliding sideways away from the metal stream of chuff. But when he attempted to straighten up, the F-4 hung, sluggish. He knew what that meant, and it wasn't good. But he wasn't pulling out now.

He let the jet pull him over now, in position for a

second burst. He came down on the right side of the airliner, in a position neither the baggage compartment nor the front of the plane could defend. He planned to come right up on the bastard and hit him point-blank, but the DC-10 was beginning to lurch from his previous attack. It was obviously damaged and might heel over on him if he came too close, so Hunter held his plane at a middle distance as he unloaded a new burst from the 30mm cannon. The right windows of the cockpit exploded inward for a split second under the bullets' impact, then outward as the plane's interior and exterior pressures equalized. The passenger plane pointed its nose at the bright Pacific and hurried down to meet it.

But the F-4 wasn't in much better shape. The right jet coughed and then gave up, and the whole plane began shuddering with irregular rhythm. Hunter turned it to the right again, but not to return to the islands. No, he was going to try to take out the other plane before he ran out of time. Trouble was, he had less time than he hoped. The second plane grew steadily in his cockpit window, but he had to fight to keep it there. The F-4 wanted to move downward, and before he could maneuver into firing range, the F-4 had its way. It began a long spiral toward the water, over which a colorless, odorless gas could well be spreading. If it were, Hunter had to pray that he'd put enough distance between his crash site and the downed DC-10, and that the prevailing winds were blowing away from him. But if that were the case, his parachute would carry him back toward the gas.

Much too aware that the *other* plane was going to get away, with no one else on its shrouded tail, Hunter waited until his spiral turned his head away from the first crash site—then yanked savagely on the ejection-sequence handle. The seat fired beneath him and he rocketed outward at an angle from the severely tilted jet. Seconds later, the automatic release ripped the seat away and popped his chute. The canopy spread and caught the air; Hunter absorbed the harsh jerk of his harness. And then he began the long, angled descent into the middle of a wet blue nowhere, with no one aware he was there at all.

Chapter 29

United Airlines flight 901 from Honolulu to San Diego
was packed like all Hawaiian flights, with every narrow seat in every narrow aisle filled. The mood on
flights headed toward the mainland was always mixed;
the passengers were happy to have spent a week or
two in the islands, wistful about leaving the beautiful
land. Other passengers were relieved to return to their
familiar lives in their familiar houses. It was the airline's job, in the persons of its overworked flight crew,
to keep them all occupied for the entire five and a
half hours. First drinks, then food, then the film, then
more drinks. Toward the end of the flight the attendants would be able to sit down, as most of the people
either dozed off or stood in line for the restrooms.

Two hours out of Honolulu on this clear Friday
morning, with the front of the cabin finished with
breakfast and the back of the cabin beginning it, the
movie was announced. Savvy passengers disdained it
because it had been edited down for airline use—it
had to be acceptable to everyone from small children
to their grandparents—but there was no way they
could avoid its effects. The flight attendants asked everyone to please pull down the shades on their tiny
windows so that the pale televised image could be
seen. If you preferred to look out on the clouds above

TALON FORCE

the bright Pacific you were begging for an annoyed reminder from your neighbor. So everyone except the truly antisocial or oblivious pulled their shades and blocked out the views.

So they missed the rockets streaking past their windows to blow their cockpit apart.

United Airlines flight 901 reminded the pilot in the DC-10 behind it of a chicken with its head cut off. The jets were still firing but there was no one to guide them. The interior pressure exploding out the missing front of the fuselage carried with it the passengers who had not had their seat belts fastened, and every piece of paper and clothing now loose inside the maelstrom of the plane. Then the depressurized interior gulped the thin air it was roaring through at six hundred miles per hour, slowing the plane with its drag. UAL 901 wobbled, wavered, and then began to turn. It went into a spin and dropped like a stone.

Anyone still alive inside got to watch the water rushing up at them for thirty-one thousand feet.

The pilot in the DC-10 preferred not to watch. It was one thing to shoot a big target; it was another to see people fall out of it and so be reminded of all the people who were still inside. Better to think of it as just a job.

"UAL nine-oh-one, this is Honolulu."

It was his cockpit radio, now locked onto the exact frequency the downed plane had been using. With a voice that trembled only slightly, he answered, "Roger, Honolulu."

"Regarding your report of another aircraft on your radar, be advised that we also thought we saw something, but it is not there now. Do you still have a reading?"

"That's a negative, Honolulu. I did just experience a wind shear so I suspect it was just a weather-related bogie."

"Roger, UAL nine-oh-one. But you are on the edge of our coverage area, and we are also experiencing an as-yet undefined problem with communications from Kauai, so we're a little busy back here. Would advise you keep an eye on your own radar, and check with San Diego control as well."

"Roger, Honolulu. Thanks a lot. UAL nine-oh-one out."

"Honolulu out."

The pilot heaved a sigh of relief. It was very quiet in his cockpit at this altitude, nearly halfway across the vast expanse of the Pacific. Maybe it was the lingering sight of those other people falling to their deaths, but he felt very alone.

He envied the other plane that had taken off with him this morning. They had a three-man crew. He had protested it; surely they should give him one man from that crew and have two two-man teams. But you really only needed one man for a mission like this, and those three were family who wanted to die together.

The pilot touched a button on the small device nestled beside the empty co-pilot's seat and felt an answering boom in his fuselage.

Outside, the straps holding the metal sheath around his plane broke loose, and it fell away toward the ocean. For a few moments the pilot had to exercise his considerable skill to deal with the sudden drag, until the metal had been completely torn away from the six-hundred-mile-an-hour wind stream.

Now his DC-10 revealed its true colors to the empty sky: the familiar colors of a United Airlines passenger jet.

UAL 901 was back on track for San Diego.

Chapter 30

Three members of TALON Force, along with Iniki, drove their Hawaiian War Canoe south along the coast like a freight train, sweating in the morning sun. Iniki chanted the pace, as fast as he dared—until the rowers told him to pick it up. As they worked their oars, stroke after stroke after stroke, they kept their ears alert for news from the back of the canoe. That was where Travis and Sam knelt, interrogating their revived prisoner.

They had taken the Chinese, strapped his hands together behind his back with plastic bonds and put another around his neck, then headed back out toward the coast as fast as they could. The Triad member had thought he might slow them down right up until the first time he tried it, when Travis, holding his leash, simply yanked him forward on his face and Jack helped haul him, choking and strangling, through the undergrowth. The man yelped and howled, but it wasn't until he hit his head on a hidden rock and passed out that they stopped and manhandled him the rest of the way.

They made their way back over the ridges and came at last to the beach where their canoe waited. Travis held the prisoner aside as the others shoved the boat back into the water. The prisoner, now awake thanks to a few slaps, was very nervous because he knew the worst was still to come. TALON Force and Iniki clambered in, then Travis led his man after them and shoved him into the back. The prisoner tumbled unceremoniously over the side, unable to break his fall with his hands strapped behind his back. His chin bounced on the flooring. It was definitely not going to get better for him anytime soon.

So it was that they surged down the coast, Travis working on extracting information. As he'd told Sarah back on Kamasho Island, he was no stranger to the art of interrogation. Before they were halfway home he had what he needed, thanks to some effective small-digit manipulation.

According to their prisoner, the Triad had found itself pushed hard after the takeover of Hong Kong. They had built themselves into a major presence in the fifteen years before that, operating along the border between the colony and the People's Republic. Smuggling anything they could profit from, in whatever direction the profit lay, had made them rich and widely feared. They had worked long and hard to build their sphere of influence, and had grown accustomed to its effect; quite often the simple mention of their name would get them what they wanted, without their having to lift a finger. But with the elimination of the border, they faced Communist authorities all the time, and Communist authorities had zero tolerance for Triads. They had built a massively secure base (Travis laughed in his face at that one), but Communists were Communists. They never gave up. It became clear all too soon that the Ch'u Triad would have to go into another line of work.

So they turned to Sarin. As the prisoner told Sam through swollen lips, once he began to talk freely, "Everyone else had banned nerve agents. If we made it *our* weapon, we would be the brokers of a hellstorm the likes of which the world has never seen."

"Then why didn't you announce yourselves after the attacks in Tokyo?"

"Because they were only a diversion. We drew international attention to the Asian side of the Pacific, so we could stage the real attack on the American side. So many top medical and law enforcement officials gathered in Tokyo meant so few looking anywhere else."

"The Air Force will take care of those planes."

"No. I don't know why—my men and I were kept away from the landing strip crew. They keep each cell on a need-to-know basis, like the Communists we battled for so long. But the word was that no one would be able to stop them."

"Why?"

"I don't know!"

"Are they operating on their own, or are they under someone's control? Say . . . Norman Pin Wong?"

"Who?"

"Isn't he the head of the Ch'u Triad?"

"I don't know. I only know Mr. Wu."

"*Knew* Mr. Wu. So who's in charge of this operation?"

"The central control area is at the jamming center. It is on a high peak in the center of the island, high enough to blanket all of Kauai, and more. There is a building up there the commanding crew can use. They say they will hide in the rain. I don't know what that means."

"I can guess. What's the strength of that crew?"

"I don't know. They keep each cell separate."

Travis paused to think as the canoe rowed on.

Chapter 31

Polihale State Park, awash with happy families playing around picnic blankets and an occasional body surfer, was coming into view as the team made its final plans.

"He said the other group was on the 'high peak,' with a building," Travis told Iniki. "Is that what you called the 'wettest spot on earth'?"

"Waialeale. It would have to be. There's actually a higher peak, Kawaikini, a little to the south, but the rain and the building are on Waialeale." Lips tight in a disapproving frown, he added, "The building he's talking about is a sacred place—*Ka'awako heiau,* which because of its location at the height of the rain marks a supreme pilgrimage."

"We'll need a chopper to get up there."

"You can have it. But you won't be able to fly all the way."

"Why not?"

"The clouds are too thick. You'll hit zero visibility long before you reach it."

"What kind of pilots do you have here?"

"Damn good ones, Major. You're invited to fly the chopper yourself if you doubt it. But you'll come to the same conclusion we all have. Once you near the peaks, you can't see a thing and the winds become extremely treacherous. The storm up there is continuous and violent, as three thousand miles of weather runs head-on into the mountain. We can get within three miles of the peak—two and a half if we're lucky. Then we can take the Halepaakai Stream trail up to the top."

Travis checked his watch. "Three miles. That should be doable, in the time we have. If not, we can target them from below."

"Major . . . if it comes to that, certainly. But Wai-aleale is a very holy spot—"

"I understand and I'll do everything I can to make certain it's untouched. But how holy will it be if tens of thousands of people die just to preserve it?"

The canoe pulled strongly into Nohili Point, where they were met by Colonel Alvarez. "Communications have gone out, as I'm sure you know," said the base commander. "I had no idea when you'd return so I just set up camp on the beach and waited."

"We know communications are out and we know why. We're going to take care of it if you can get us to a chopper at once."

"You got it, Major."

TALON Force leapt into Alvarez's pickup, which then churned away across the sand, snaking its way onto the road leading back to the center of the base.

"What's the communication situation look like from this end?" Travis asked.

"Everything's screwed up. Jamming's been perfected after long practice against the Voice of America, but this is cranked up so high it's probably giving everyone on the island cancer. The problem is, we can't pinpoint the source because our equipment's jammed."

"That's not a problem. We know where to go. But what about telephone and Internet lines?"

"It all goes out through the Lihue center, and a bomb went off there just before the jamming began. Last I heard, the cops had no suspects, but I guess you do. Anyway, the lines are down for at least eight hours."

"All right," said Travis. "Here's what you've got to do. Have somebody fly to Honolulu. If they're jammed, too, he should land wherever he has to. We have to get a message to the States. The Ch'u Triad has sent two planes disguised as commercial airliners toward the West Coast. Each plane is carrying a Sarin bomb."

"They won't get through. The planes won't have any flight plans registered—"

"They'll be challenged, sure. But what happens then? There's a good chance they'll be allowed to land so things can get straightened out, and that's all they'll need. The Air Force has to be warned!"

"I'll send my best pilot right away."

"Meantime, we need your best chopper pilot to take my team and Major Palauea as close to Waiaieale as we can get. The head of the Triad is up there in a *heiau.*"

Alvarez routed the pilots out of the mess hall himself. The Honolulu-bound pilot was Captain Cindy Saunders, a harsh-eyed redhead with a deep Southern drawl. The chopper pilot was Captain Lou Schultz, who appeared to have only three fingers on his left hand. Within five minutes each was briefed and ready for his mission. Travis gave Saunders her final briefing.

"With luck you'll escape the jamming range before you even get to Honolulu. Try the radio as soon as you get airborne. After you get the stateside planes scrambled, tell the Honolulu people to look for one of my crew, Captain Hunter Blake. He went after the airliners in an F-4. I don't know how much fuel his plane had, so he may not be able to follow all the way to the coast. The DC-10s also may have taken exception to his being on their tails. The Air Force may have to do a search and rescue."

"I understand, Major," Captain Saunders said, saluting crisply. "Hunter Blake is a little bit of a legend in the service. I've never met the man, but I'll make sure I do."

"Good luck."

She climbed into her F-14 Tomcat and taxied onto the runway so quickly that she lifted her left wheel off the tarmac. The jets revved, then she launched herself down the straightaway and soared smoothly into the morning blue.

Just then a handheld surface-to-air missile rocketed out from the hills behind the base and blew her from the skies.

As the people on the shore looked on in horror, Captain Saunders's jet became a blooming fireball, as hunks of twisted metal arced into the shimmering sea.

"You called it, Travis," breathed Jen. "A perfect spot for an ambush."

Alvarez ran to his men, who were already pouring from the mess hall in response to the sound of the explosion. From across the grassy expanse, TALON Force could see the agitation and urgency in the man's body language. Two units immediately headed for the hills while three others manned their own missile launchers and trained them on the location from which the rocket was fired. While the first teams were making their way into the foothills and up the slopes, the second teams peppered the area Alvarez pointed out as being the source of the attack. If they had their way, the first teams would find nothing but a charred hole in the ground when they got up there. If they didn't, they were determined to protect the next take-offs. Without knowing precisely what was going on, they understood that they couldn't let their facility be shut down.

Alvarez ran back to Travis. "Get going, Major! I'll send another pilot to Honolulu. I'll send the whole base if I have to."

Captain Schultz stepped forward. "I've had a little experience with missiles, Major Barrett. I'll get you where you need to go."

Travis nodded. "Let's do it."

The five members of TALON Force Eagle Team, along with Iniki, clambered into the AH-64A Apache. The turbine began to whine, the rotor blades began to whip, and each passenger sat in one of the open side doorways, their XM-29 Smart Rifles at the ready. They would be relatively useless unless they were a lot closer to the missile launcher than they wanted to be, but the simple act of preparation added to their sense that they would prevail against the Triad.

Schultz raised the Apache just two feet off the ground, then turned in place and moved away toward the water, away from the dangerous hills. A hundred yards out he made a sharp left turn and motored toward the south, barely above the waves. But the missile launcher in the distance spoke again. Like the man in Kai Tak Airport, members of the Ch'u Triad appeared to have little respect for their own lives if they could accomplish their mission. The shot from the hills was immediately answered with a barrage from the base.

But the missile was on its way toward the chopper. Schultz's reactions were honed to survival in the air. He couldn't go down so he went up, banking sharply to the sky. The missile, coming in from a distance, passed under the Apache's fuselage with just two feet to spare.

Schultz jammed his foot against the left pedal to spin the chopper back toward the hills. The nose veered downward and the tail shot up as he pushed it directly toward his opponent. Though he had he utmost respect for the missile launcher, he was tired of playing cat and mouse. The thought flashed through Travis's mind to order a retreat, but it never turned into words. He appreciated Schultz's spirit, and sometimes you just had to ride your hunch.

Another missile came flying out of the jungle. Almost contemptuously Schultz tilted hard over and dove, letting the rocket flash by. Again, it didn't miss by much. Still tilted over, he pulled his spring-away gunsight in front of his face and tromped the floor-mounted trigger to his .50-caliber machine guns. The red tracers ran up the hillside, spewing broken branches, and crossed the spot where he estimated the shooter to be. As the Apache came into position, he pulled his own missile launch, putting three 2.75-inch rockets into the trees.

Abruptly he turned his 'copter skyward again. If his attack hadn't worked he needed to make himself and his passengers scarce. But nobody shot back at them now. The field teams would determine if he'd taken out his target. It was time to get back to the mission at hand.

Lieutenant Alfred Burlingkamp picked up speed and lifted his F-14 Tomcat into the Hawaiian sky, following the same flight path as Cindy Saunders. His face was wooden as he waited to react to whatever might happen. The sky was pale blue above, the sea a deep turquoise below. A flock of seabirds floated out across the water far down the coast. A tanker from the far east made a black blotch on the horizon.

No one fired at him.

He banked the Tomcat toward Honolulu, but not without a long salute to the memory of his fallen comrade.

Chapter 32

The weather near the Waialeale peak was everything
Iniki had said it would be, and worse. Even getting
within three miles turned out to be impossible. It was
more like three and a half, down on what Schultz
called the Kaluahaula Ridge, where they hovered next
to a bubbling stream. They couldn't see more than
twenty feet ahead when the Apache finally had to
land. The gray fog blew briskly down from the mountaintop. A night hike had been a challenge, but a day
hike in an enveloping fog was going to be worse.

And at the same time, it was strangely pleasant,
temperature-wise. They were only at four thousand
feet now, headed for five; the fog provided a cool
blanket. After all they'd been through, it was damn
refreshing. They'd switched from their luau clothes to
long pants and sleeves on the flight up, but it really
wasn't necessary. Even with the sun completely hidden, they could have climbed this Hawaiian mountain
in just shorts.

Still, at the end of it all, it wasn't the sort of day
that your average tourist, or even your average back-
country hiker, said, "Let's get up there." The thick
fog spun and twisted on the exposed ridge, and there
was little chance of sightseeing. The vegetation was
scrubby but full: small, twisted trees, ferns, and plants

bursting with red flowers, and running through it all was a path of the ubiquitous red mud. But twenty feet in any direction there was only gray fog.

"Nice day for an ambush," muttered Jack to Iniki. "And if we know anything about the Ch'u Triad by now, they'll have one waiting. I'm pulling point on this, Travis."

Travis nodded. "Iniki, you and I will head the group behind him. You don't have a Micro-Biochip implant like we do, so I'll clue you to anything I get, and you can use me to tell the group anything you need to."

"Actually," said Iniki, "I've got half an idea about that. Give me a minute." He went back over to Schultz at the Apache and engaged in a quick, intense discussion. Both men were waving their hands in the fog, evidently trying to come to some meeting of the minds. Evidently, they did. They shook hands and Schultz climbed back into the chopper.

"Godspeed, gentleman and ladies!" Schultz called, then put the machine in the air and vanished into the mist.

Iniki came back to the team. They set off along the trail at a trot, spreading out as much as they could. Sometimes the trail widened to fifteen, even twenty feet; other times it shrank to force them into a single file. And sometimes the trot became a slog, as brooks slid across the trail and turned it to red quickmud. Everywhere they looked there was either water, lush plant life, or fog—and it was only going to get worse.

Lieutenant Burlingkamp was halfway to Honolulu when he broke through the radio jamming and made contact. The air shuttles from Kauai had already reported the radio outage, but this was the first Hickam Air Force Base had heard of the renegade airliners, or Captain Hunter Blake's F-4. The message was immediately forwarded to Air Force centers on the West Coast, and Air-Sea Rescue went up to look for the man missing in three thousand miles of blue water.

Chapter 33

After twenty minutes, TALON Force came upon a second trail, leading upward more steeply to the right. Iniki told Travis that was the way to go. Had they continued in the direction they'd been traveling, they'd have entered what looked to be a swamp, sodden with the runoff from above, and it soon became clear that the new trail ran alongside the swamp. When they'd hiked down in the valley last night, they'd had troubles slipping on the mud, but nothing like they encountered here. Jack led the way as surefootedly as anyone could, and the others tried to walk in his deep footprints. But their long pants and shirts were solidly covered in red smears and streaks before they'd covered the first mile. If they'd had the option to slow down, or not take this trail at all, they'd gladly have done so. But they didn't have that option.

"That is the Alakai Swamp," Iniki told Travis. "The continual rain up above has seven nice channels for runoff—seven rivers—but even they can't take all the water. So the rest of it seeps down this side and turns the ground to slime."

"I never saw a swamp run downhill," said Jack.

"You ever been to the Louisiana bayous, or the Florida Everglades?" Iniki asked.

"I was born in N'awlins—spent time down in the

bayous when I'd visit my cousins, but I grew up in Atlanta."

"Well, swamps are flat there because the land near the water is flat. Here, the land near the water—rain water, not ocean water—isn't."

"Why doesn't the whole thing slide down to the valleys, then?"

"The rain tends to fall off on the far side. This side just gets the fog."

"Well," said Jack, "just so long as there aren't any gators on this mountain."

"What I don't understand," said Jennifer, "is why is this trail so primitive, if we're in a state park?"

"We're not, Lieutenant. First, everything to our right is public land, and everything to our left is a wilderness preserve. Second, Kauai is proud to be part of an American state, but it is still Hawaiian. People here don't want the well-tended trails of the national parks; they want things to stay the way they've always been. Nature rules this island."

"Just one tram ride to the top wouldn't have hurt anybody."

Jack suddenly dropped his hand authoritatively. The team hit the ground as one.

"What've you got, Jack?" hissed Travis.

"Fresh mud on the trail. Somebody's been in and out of the swamp here within the past ten minutes."

Before Travis could answer, another answer erupted from their left: the blast of an RPG-7 anti-tank rocket launcher. The brilliance of the burst obliterated the fog's gray embrace as the 85mm rocket flew a foot above the trail, just above the flattened Americans.

Their opponents were dug in over there, ready for them as they came up the path, but considering all that TALON Force had done to them so far, they'd maybe given them too much respect. They'd set themselves up far enough from the trail that TALON Force would have had to go another twenty yards for the perfect ambush. As it was they had a little bit of ground cover, afforded by a little bit of rise. What advantage the Triad troopers might have had from being farther up the slope was negated by their desire to hunker down off the trail. They'd ended up more or less level with the Americans.

This was going to come down to weaponry and marksmanship because neither side could charge the other—not through that muck. And for once, TALON Force was outgunned. They had the XM-29 Smart Rifles but the Ch'u Triad had their now-familiar rocket-propelled grenade launcher, and from the sound of it, Tek-9s along with their AK-47s. Neither of the rifles was as advanced as the XM-29, but they were deadly enough.

Travis, Iniki, and Sam rolled left, down into the swampy mud, firing as they went. Jen and Sarah crawled to the right for a better angle. Jack stayed right where he was, in a muddy depression right on the trail. The fog blew across the swamp, alternately hiding and revealing their positions.

Jack stared down at the red mud and blinked until the retina echo of the RPG blast faded against the dark background. Bullets were flying past him but he needed to see in order to aim effectively. Just as he cleared his vision, the tracers from the swamp marched right up to his hole, but couldn't make the angle to hit the man inside. The shooter was just too low. Frustrated, he turned his attention to the women in the brush—and that was when Jack threw his torso upward with one thrust of his powerful stomach muscles. His head and arms popped up above the lip of the mud hole, his elbows dropped onto the muck, and he tore off a full clip of 5.56mm shells. He had no time to use the Smart Rifle's millimeter wave sensor and aiming device; he had to settle for brute force. The Triad member with the RPG and three of his friends fell forward in the muck. It wasn't pretty, but it was effective The Triad had picked their spot and almost achieved surprise, but TALON Force drew first blood. After Tokyo, after the Chinese bunker, the Ch'u Triad had to be wondering if they even had the simple *ability* to stop TALON Force.

As others returned fire, Jack was already back down in his hole.

Meanwhile, the women in the brush had been forgotten, so it was their turn to go to work. Both Sarah and Jen activated their own grenade launchers on their XM-29s—manually, not with a flick of an eye beneath the Battle Sensor Devices they no longer had—and triggered them.

The 20mm grenades sailed side-by-side into the swamp and landed five feet apart, just in front of a nest of Ch'us. The men were behind a low hillock of mud, but the grenades burst into hundreds of tiny, razor-sharp fragments of shrapnel that cut straight through the hill. Sarah and Jennifer never saw their opponents but they did hear them scream and die.

Even as the screams were fading, the fog abruptly thickened. Without stopping to think, the way a more seasoned warrior would have, Sam jumped up and moved with the gray screen to find a more effective firing point. Travis, firing steadily, told him through the Micro-Biochip Transmitter to come back, but Sam was caught up in an idea he had. Being lighter than the others, he didn't sink as deep into the swamp mud as they would have. Still, his progress was more "wading" than "running." His feet, gripped by the muck, made sucking sounds as he moved. Bullets flew from the fog, drawn by the noises, but they were well wide of their target; the fog distorted all sound. But the swarm of lead was enough to alert Sam to the fact that maybe invisibility wasn't enough, so he threw himself back to the ground—and right on top of a Triad trooper crawling to better his own position. Sam would tell it differently later, of course, but it was mostly luck that found the barrel of the Smart Rifle pressed against the trooper's ear. Sam squeezed the trigger and that meeting was history.

At the same time, Iniki was showing both the Chinese and the mainlanders what a lifetime of experience was worth. Inspired by Sam's recklessness but far more savvy, he had slid forward across the swamp like a water moccasin, his arms, legs, and torso all flat to the ground. When the fog cleared for a moment, he was ten feet from the shredded hillock Sarah and Jen had destroyed. With the fog wrapped around him like a cloak, he darted forward. Ten feet later, the red mud was awash with crimson blood, but still he kept his chin in it until he reached an RPG-7 launcher. As far as he could tell, this one hadn't had a chance to be used before its owner died; the question was whether TALON Force grenades had left it in operating condition. Only one way to find out. He got his legs up underneath him and waited patiently for the fog to reveal an enemy. When it did he saw three Triad troopers moving away from him, hoping to sneak up and surprise the enemy. The RPG was overkill so he reluctantly put it aside and used his Smart Rifle. He successfully activated the aiming device, and three smart bullets did their work.

Then there was silence.

Was that the end of the Triad ambushers? The line-of-sight signals flew from TALON member to TALON member, while Iniki patiently sat and waited. No one saw any movement from any of the locations they had spotted attacks coming from. But in the fog it was hard to be absolutely certain what those locations had been. This would have been a perfect time and place for the Automatic Battlefield Motion Sensor built into the Battle Ensembles, or the thermal viewing capability of the BSDs. But denied that luxury, they had to rely on their eyes and ears.

"TALON." Travis's voice again sounded in the team members' ears. "Iniki showed me how to work this swamp. Sarah and I will crawl forward from opposite sides. Sam, work your way toward Iniki—he's fifteen meters back toward the trail. Tell him what's up and then both of you scout your area. Jack, Jen, stay ready to cover us. Go."

It took ten minutes to be certain the area was secured—ten minutes they could ill afford but could not avoid. In the end they were certain there were no more ambushers.

"There's no way to know if we killed them all, or if some escaped," said Travis, "but we'll have to assume that the Triad has some means of communication among themselves and radioed upstairs that we're coming. We're going to have to be doubly alert as we go higher."

"If you don't mind, Major . . ." said Iniki.

"Got an idea?"

"I do. It's what I was talking to Schultz about. It was to be expected that the Ch'u Triad would set an ambush along the trail; I just didn't know where. But now that they may have established our route—let's bag the trail and cut through the swamp."

"Can we do that?"

"It won't be a whole lot worse than the trail. It's only two miles from here to the top. We can make pads for our feet from the vegetation, the way we did when I was a kid. It's like using snowshoes—a lattice of branches wrapped in grass and vines, tied to the bottom of our boots. We couldn't do it on the trail but it'll be perfect for the Alakai." Iniki's eyes were lighting up at the thought. "I used to play up here a lot. I'm used to this terrain and we can avoid the worst spots. We can make a direct line for *Kaawako heiau* without worrying about another ambush. And the Ch'u Triad will never expect us to come that way."

Chapter 34

Danny Walling, air traffic controller at San Diego International, worked his way through the dozens of aircraft approaching his city. It was another gorgeous day in Southern California, but Danny, as usual, wasn't really aware of it. His eyes were glued to the green circular screen that showed several moving blips.

Walling had worked for a time up the coast at LAX, with six months along the way at Burbank, but San Diego was his favorite by far. The airport there is practically in the heart of the city. Planes came in low right over the downtown office buildings and high-rise apartments. The only other place he'd personally seen with a similar need for precision and competence in its ATC crews was San Jose. But the airport up there had been on the outskirts of the city until the explosive growth of the Silicon Valley had eaten up all the intervening ground. Now there were miles and miles of those two-story office buildings with wide green lawns surrounding the airport, so if somebody screwed up and misdirected a jumbo jet up there, they could kill a lot of Coke-swilling code junkies—and probably, to be fair, deal a significant blow to the computer industry. But down here in San Diego, a similar mishap could destroy whole corporate centers. So all in all, it'd just be better not to have any mishaps at all.

"UAL nine-oh-one."

"Roger UAL nine-oh-one."

"Request clearance for landing."

"Be advised, there will be a delay of fifteen minutes. Fog at SFO delayed flights out of there this morning. Go to one-niner-five at one-seven-thousand for three minutes, then turn two-seven-oh for seven minutes. Will advise further at that time."

"Um, I'd rather . . . well, all right."

"Problem, UAL nine-oh-one?"

"No, San Diego." But the pilot didn't seem certain. Then he blurted out: "Is there any other reason for the delay?"

Danny was surprised; United pilots were usually among the calmest he encountered. But maybe the guy had a hot date. It *was* Friday, after all. "No other reason, UAL nine-oh-one. I say again, do you have a problem?"

"No. Going to one-niner-five at one-seven-thousand for three minutes, then turn two-seven-oh for seven minutes. UAL nine-oh-one out."

The dialogue was odd enough that Danny might have wondered about it—if he'd had the time. But air traffic controllers never have any to spare. He turned his attention to the next blip on his screen, already thinking ahead to the one after that.

Chapter 35

The five members of TALON Force were getting used to the Alakai Swamp.

The pads Iniki had showed them how to make with simple Hawaiian ingenuity were working perfectly, just like snowshoes, as he'd said. Their weight was now spread out and diffused atop the thick mud. The branches in the pads broke beneath their weight but were held in place by the sinewy grass and vines, so the whole mess became molded to their feet. Though the mud was thick, they could work their way across it without sinking into the soup.

Iniki seemed to know every twist and turn in what was an almost featureless landscape. There were trees, hills, even a series of abandoned, weathered telephone poles marching across the gray marshes at one point. But the ground beneath their feet all looked the same, and that ground made up most of what there was to see. That, and the swirling fog. Without a guide who'd grown up here, they'd have had a rough go of it.

Jack, now second in line, moved up beside the Hawaiian. "How do you do it?" he wondered.

"Can you find your way around Atlanta?"

"Sure, but Atlanta's got street signs."

"Can you find your way around St. Joe, Missouri?"

"I've never been to St. Joe, Missouri."

"But it's got street signs." Iniki grinned. "Look, Captain—"

"Jack."

"Okay, Jack. This island is twenty-five miles by thirty-three. You can drive as far as you can drive around it in ninety minutes if you're serious about it. You could drive up and down every road in the place in a day or two. After that you start hiking. And when you hike on Kauai, you don't just put in your time. You see valleys, waterfalls, beaches, peaks, *views*— everything you need to make you want to go find some more of it tomorrow. So, you grew up in Atlanta and you learned your neighborhood, and then the best routes to the Braves games—"

"Hawks."

"—and over to your girl's house, and pretty soon you knew a lot about getting around Atlanta that you didn't strictly *need* to know. You put the city inside your brain. Well, I've got this island in my brain. I've been pretty much everywhere, except maybe the penthouse suites in the Princeville resorts." He gestured at the empty landscape. "I've never taken this route we're on today, but I know the lay of the land, I know the direction the fog comes from. Trust me. We're going to come out in the perfect spot to catch the Ch'u Triad asleep at the switch."

Jack spoke into his neck implant. "Hey Travis, you know what Sun Tzu wrote in *The Art of War*? 'One who does not employ local guides cannot gain advantages of terrain.'" Jack chuckled, an eerie sound vibrating in TALON Force's necks. "Sun Tzu knew it all, man!"

TALON Force and their local guide continued to make their way across the Alakai Swamp. They were gradually climbing, but not anywhere nearly as steeply as they had been on the Waialae Trail; it was clear that they were circling around the base of the peak. But eventually they were going to have to make up the difference, and when that time came, Travis was almost flattered by Iniki's opinion of their ability to do it. Coming around a grove of scrub trees and ferns, the mist suddenly parted to reveal a sixty-foot waterfall, tumbling beautiful and alone into a river falling away to the north.

"Top of that," said Iniki, cheerfully, "and we're almost there."

The fog, augmented by the mist from the falling water, immediately closed up again.

"Well," drawled Travis, "Stan and Hunter went down a fifty-foot elevator shaft to rescue us, so we should be able to climb sixty feet."

"Hell," laughed Iniki, "you don't have to go up it like salmon going to spawn. There's a climbing path along the side of it—rocks to hold onto."

"If you can do it, we can do it."

"Then let's do it."

Iniki led them into a muddy basin beside the river. The mire made it feel like they were slogging through jello for the next ten minutes, as the wall of rock that framed the falls grew gradually nearer. When Iniki reached the waterfall, he sat and removed the pads of sticks and vines, then stuck his boots in the foaming pool to wash the red mud away. The rest of the team followed suit. "It's gonna be slippery whatever we do, but the mud would make it worse," he said.

Sam looked upward, but saw only shifting mist. "Didn't some people get killed at a falls in Hawaii when boulders came loose and fell on them?"

"Sure. Happens all the time. Rocks falling, at least—not people getting killed. Like I told Jen, we let Kauai be Kauai."

"You talk about the island like it's alive."

Iniki was astonished. "Of course she's alive. Pele, over on the Big Island, is the Queen now, but Kauai was the first queen, and she's never died."

"I'm not much into that kind of thinking," said Sam.

"That's why you choose to sit in a room full of electrical currents when you could be hiking in the rain forest," said Sarah, finding a spot to sit nearby and then leaning forward to rinse her boots. "*I* certainly feel the life force here."

"Aw, Sarah, I didn't mean . . ."

She patted his shoulder. "I know exactly what you meant. The scientific mind: it's very good at cutting away the irrational from the rational until everything can be explained."

"But that's how we learn," Sam protested.

"Is it?" Sarah asked, rubbing water on her face now. "That worked for a long time, as science worked its way down from elements to molecules to atoms to protons, neutrons, and electrons. But now we *learn* that below that, nothing is really predictable the way science always defined it. Below that level it's all probabilities, where waves are particles and particles are waves. In other words," she concluded, straightening, "the scientific mind has worked its way back from the rational to the irrational. There is always *something* underneath everything we see that defies our explanations."

"So far," said Sam stubbornly. "But we keep learning. As you say, we've come a long way, and there's no reason to think we've reached the end. Hell, we're at the start of a new millennium—"

"Our knowledge will change, but nature never will."

"Okay, kiddies, let's table the nature of the universe and set our minds to this cliff," interrupted Travis. "It may not really exist or it may be the petrified hair of a goddess, but it's still between us and our objective."

The others made certain their Smart Rifles were strapped tightly across their backs so they wouldn't swing loose while climbing, then got in line.

Iniki lacked their precisely honed commando skills but had the familiarity of a native. He started out almost leaping from foothold to foothold like a mountain goat, but soon was using his hands and feet like everyone behind him.

The last four hundred yards were the toughest:

solid, slippery mud, running almost completely vertically over solid rock, defied purchase. There were
rough handholds: a tree root here, a foot-sized ledge
there. But the fog was total and squalls of rain burst
over the ridgetop just above, making the roots and
ledges as slippery as ice on Christmas.

When TALON Force had all reached the top, they
could hardly see each other through the mist, let alone
where to go next. It was then that Iniki took a small
metallic device from his rucksack. Small earphones,
like those on a Walkman, snapped free and were
placed on his head; a small mike dropped in front of
his mouth.

"It's not what you guys use," he smiled, "but it's
the standard-issue equivalent. And it's a lot more useful right here and right now."

He clipped the device to his belt so his hands were
free, then flipped a switch on its front. "Moa Nest,
this is Moa-7. Do you copy?"

"We copy, Moa-7," answered a voice in his ear.

"We're on the roof, but we came the back way."

"Hang on while I zero in on you."

Sam asked, "Who are you talking to?"

"Schultz," said Iniki. "We're making line-of-sight
laser communication. Radio waves are jammed but
light isn't, so he flew around to Kalaluanahelehele—"

"Kalalalaboom-de-ay?" said Sam.

"How in the hell can you remember these names?"
demanded Jennifer.

"Just be satisfied that you don't have to." Iniki said.
"It's a peak to the south, a thousand feet below this
one, but on a clear line of sight all along our route
up here. He's got a Geological Survey topo map and
he'll guide us the rest of the way. It's only a quarter
mile, but considering that we're flying almost blind,
we need outside eyes."

"Why? Where are we going?"

The Hawaiian pointed at the enveloping fog. There
was nothing else to see. "A path, right along the edge

of a cliff. One wrong step and it's a thousand feet to the bottom." He seemed very cheerful at the prospect.

Schultz's voice sounded in his ear. "Are you at the end of the drainpipe, up there on the roof?"

"You got it, Moa Nest."

"All right. Make sure you birds stay tight. You're going to want to move north-northeast, bearing seventeen-point . . . six. I repeat, seventeen-point-six."

"Seventeen-point-six. I copy."

"Exactly twenty-three of your gallumphing foot-steps, Moa-7."

"We'll see." Iniki turned to the others. "Okay, Schultz is going to guide me, and I'll guide you. Line up behind me, single file and as close as your long associations will let you. I'd choose one of the ladies to follow me but I suppose I'll get Travis. Then you will all do exactly what the person in front of you does. If you could see this trail you'd probably get vertigo, but consider it a blessing that you can't."

"Lead on, Iniki. We'll follow every move you make."

"And don't make any unnecessary noise—not because you'll scare the Triad, because even if they hear you they won't be able to figure out where the sound's coming from. But I need to count, so don't disturb me."

The big Hawaiian waited until they were lined up tight behind him, each one's hands on the shoulders of the one in front of him, then used his compass to double-check his bearing. He drew a deep breath and looked at the featureless fog in front of them. Then he began to stride carefully forward: "One . . . two . . . three . . ."

When he got to twenty-two, he stopped, then, holding onto Travis right behind him, reached out a foot for twenty-three. His foot reached air, before settling down onto a steep slope. He smiled, putting no weight on the foot, and pulled himself back, dragging the foot up the slope.

"Moa Nest, that works out to twenty-two-point-five gallumphs on the ground."

"Copy, Moa-7. I'll take that into account. Now, you want to turn left, bearing three-four-one, for . . . call it five-point-five steps."

"*You* can call it whatever the hell you want to call it! Just don't give me any approximations!"

"Five-point-five. That's affirmative. Won't happen again."

Iniki spoke to the group once more. "We're going to make a turn exactly where I'm standing. We're going just a little distance—not enough for all of you to make the turn before we stop again. Who's back there?" He peered into the mist, which thinned momentarily. "Jack. Keep your head on straight, buddy. You're going to be in a different time zone from the rest of us."

"You just worry about yourself, fat boy."

"Like I said, it won't bother me if you fall off," grinned Iniki. "Just be sure you let go when you do. So okay, here we go."

They moved forward, shuffling like a six-sectioned caterpillar, for five-and a half paces. Iniki was pleased to see that the number was exactly right. He got the next set of instructions and they moved slowly onward. They really couldn't see a damn thing; without a voice from the clear they'd have slipped and fallen to their deaths half a dozen times.

As it was, they were ten minutes into their journey when Sarah put a foot down just to the left of those before her in line and found nothing beneath it. She lurched sideways, trying to get a foothold. Travis and Sam, before her and behind her, braced themselves; Sam had his hands on her shoulders and she still clutched Travis. She was so light her momentum didn't budge Travis at all.

"Easy there, nature girl," he said. "Just use me to get back up."

With Sam's help, Sarah pulled herself back onto the path. Then they went on.

The trek seemed interminable, though it was just a little more than half an hour. There were no other mishaps, but the slow, deliberate pace of it set the team's teeth on edge. They'd been racing toward a climax in this mission for so long that taking it one step at a time made them all antsy.

But at last Iniki's voice floated back: "We're here. And the ridge opens out. Step on up."

They moved forward through the mist, like ghosts.

"What we came for is around the next turn—there," Iniki said, holding his pointing finger out at about a two o'clock angle. They could barely see his finger. But a few moments later, the continually churning currents in the weather opened a gap and they saw, for a second, the turning, and the plateau beyond it. A small grove of trees offered a hiding place. "Get into position and look straight ahead, about a hundred feet and up maybe ten feet." They moved forward, cautiously, peering through the empty gray void. Soon another gap in the fog momentarily blew open and they could see a wooden structure—*Kaawako heiau*. It sat atop a rise, seemingly at the tip of the world, and two Chinese, wearing hooded parkas against the weather, stood guard. They were facing the other way—toward the path TALON Force had abandoned for the swamp.

"The most sacred *heiau* on Kauai," said Iniki, his voice low with respect, caution, and anger. "It's made of mahogany, brought here by the people especially to withstand this climate."

"There's a light on inside," said Travis equally softly.

"They've got electricity," said Sarah. "Hear the gasoline generator hum?"

"For their communications with the planes."

"Yes," Iniki agreed, his voice hardening. "All the

comforts of home, for someone a long way from home. Someone who doesn't belong here."

"They think they're pretty impregnable because of the trail," said Jack. "They think no one can get here. But the flip side of that is, they don't want to go out there and look, either."

"So now we show 'em what they're missing," said Jen.

"Yes. But don't forget that they could very well have Sarin," said Sarah. The rain howled, the fog shifted, but the word sat there like a whale in a bathtub. Without anything further to say, they all donned their protective gear.

Chapter 36

Inside the *Kaawako heiau,* Norman Pin Wong was comfortable. If it weren't for the occasional tendril of fog that slid through the cracks in the closed shutters, an observer might have thought the forty-eight-year-old Chinese gentleman was in the den of his summer home on the Kwangtung coast, enjoying the sound of the rain on the roof. An old chair, left by some previous visitor to the *heiau,* was draped with a colorful silk shawl to lend a homey touch. A bottle of twenty-five-year-old single-malt Scotch and a heavy crystal glass rested on the floor beside it, within easy reach. But there the illusion ended, because two thousand-watt standing spotlights were trained on the chair. They threw the rest of the room into comparative shadow, and in that shadow stood a single television camera and the men and equipment to make it work. An observer who had been to the airstrip in the valley far below or the bunker on the Chinese coast would have recognized the hallmark of the Ch'u Triad: a complete and finished job, with no regard for the human difficulties of transporting equipment to a mine shaft, a remote canyon, or a rainswept mountain top.

Norman Pin Wong was a tall, thin man, almost cadaverous. He wore a two thousand dollar Saville Row suit, vaguely presidential, tailored to provide more heft to his slight shoulders. He looked like what he was: an extremely successful multinational businessman. A modern skyscraper, designed by Parisians, towered over Hong Kong, and though most of the other businessmen who met with him there had fairly good suspicions of his other activities, no one could point to them for consorting with a *known* criminal. It has been good, thought Norman Pin Wong, for others to suspect his involvement in the Ch'u Triad; it kept them as honest as multinational businessmen ever are.

In a way, it was fitting that he now sat atop a remote corner of the world.

After the Chinese takeover of Hong Kong, Norman Pin Wong had seen the end of his own life. Not a physical end; he had never felt much fear of, or even concern with, death. No, Norman Pin Wong realized that running his business from Hong Kong would become more and more difficult as the People's Republic slowly but surely squeezed the life from the territory. They would think they were leaving it alive, because after all it was a wonderful source of income for them, but they would just *control* it a little better than the English had. And because they were totalitarian at heart, they would never understand that capitalism cannot prosper when it is *controlled*.

And if he were completely honest with himself, which Norman Pin Wong preferred to be . . . with the Chinese in charge, he could not continue to be the successful multinational scion he was.

So he would have to leave the city and the bunker in the country behind. There would be no problem moving his assets; most of them were in Switzerland and the Grand Caymans anyway. But what then? Start over? Lease a suite in Los Angeles or Toronto or Berlin and go back to the life he had known, as lucrative as it was?

No.

It was time for a new life.

As the most powerful man in the world.

July 25, 1350 hours
San Diego, California

"UAL nine-oh-one."

"Roger, San Diego."

"You are cleared for landing, on runway 22-L."

"Thank you, San Diego."

The pilot brought his DC-10 around in a wide, slow arc. Before him stretched the blue horizon. Somewhere over the edge of it, nearly halfway around the world, was his home. Well, it had been his home, for many years—a small apartment on the fourteenth floor of an off-white building in Kowloon. He had let the lease lapse when Mr. Pin Wong had given him this mission. His neighbors all knew he'd been feeling poorly; they could see it in his thinning face. They assumed he was moving to a hospital, or to the house of relatives, but anyway, they assumed he was going to die soon. And they were right. But before the cancer took him he was going to die for a purpose: one hundred thousand dollars in a bank account for his sister's children, and the honor of this final service to the Ch'u Triad, which had been his life.

The pilot turned his plane and his back on the ocean and focused on the city of San Diego ahead of him now. The procedures for dealing with air traffic control and a landing in this city had been drilled into him over a period of a week. No one could tell there was anything wrong with UAL 901.

He swept over the coastline ten miles to the south and made another turn, bringing his craft around to approach the airport from the east. He began his descent and for a moment a wave of almost unbearable nostalgia washed over him. Landing in such a crowded area was so much like landing at Kai Tak in Hong

Kong. The landscape was much flatter but you couldn't see much of it as the buildings rushed toward you. For a moment he saw people sunbathing on the roofs of the buildings in the hills leading down to the harbor and the landing strip, and he wondered what would happen if he let them live.

Shouldn't these people be able to live? Dead ahead now was Balboa Park, with the I-5 freeway just beyond it, and the airport just beyond that. If he pulled up now, he'd just go right on back out to sea.

But he would fail Mr. Pin Wong, who had provided his good life, and would provide a good life for his nephews and nieces. And Pin Wong never tolerated failures.

He crossed the freeway at one hundred feet and touched his wheels to runway 22-L in the smoothest landing he'd made in all his good life.

July 25, 1155 hours
Waialeale Peak, Kauai, Hawaii

"Mr. Pin Wong."
"Yes?"
"The airplane has landed in San Diego."
"Then I'll have Tung activate the transmitter."
Norman Pin Wong settled himself in the chair, awaiting the storm he was about to unleash.

Chapter 37

Outside the *heiau*, TALON Force, in their Level A protective suits, was ready to go. The rain was a tricky ally, because it might cover them until they were in the sentries' back pockets, or it might open up like the curtain at the theater. *Now entering, stage right, TALON Force!* They'd just have to take their chances.

But at that moment, the door to the *heiau* swung wide, throwing a solid block of yellow light into the rain, and a single man came out. He seemed in a hurry. He had a flashlight, which couldn't do him any good, and he all but ran off into the mist.

"Jack! I don't want loose cannons showing up in the middle of this action!"

It was all Travis had to say. Jack slipped away from the grove of trees, into the fog and rain. As if on cue the fog opened, revealing him completely, but no one was looking his way. He ran as fast as he could, making no noise; fortunately the moist dirt and the fall of the rain absorbed most of the sound. The problem was, he didn't know how far the guy he was following had gone. He could run up his back before he knew it.

A sentry on the far side of the plateau looked at his watch—squinting in the pale, shifting rain light. "Shouldn't the planes have arrived by now?" he asked his partner in Cantonese.

"What's it look like in the little house?" asked the other, and turned to look. As he did the rain closed in front of him; he saw neither the *heiau* nor Jack.

Dong Tung made his way up the rough ground toward a small outcropping, some twenty-five feet higher than the plateau, where he had situated a satellite uplink and generator. Tung had overseen the installation and knew that the spot they'd chosen was both an excellent one for broadcasting, but a dangerous one for him to reach on foot. The Blonder-Tongue amplifier and satellite transmitter were easily capable of cutting in on feeds through satellites in geosynchronous orbit above. When given full power they would probably make his bones glow. He bent to switch the system on and check its operation. If anything went wrong now, Mr. Pin Wong would make certain he never left this accursed mountain.

Just as his finger pushed the black plastic switch, he stiffened. He thought he heard someone coming after him. Had Mr. Pin Wong changed his mind? He had better check. Tung turned and started down the hill.

Jack heard him coming but before he knew it, Tung was in front of him; the rain had dimmed the Chinese man's footsteps just as it had Jack's, making Jack think he was farther away. He couldn't risk a shot so he lunged upward, thrusting a heavily knuckled fist at Tung's head. But Tung recoiled and Jack missed. Tung had the advantage and took it, chopping at Jack's head with his heavy flashlight. But Jack anticipated the move and dodged, even as he swung his legs around to cut Tung's feet out from under him. Tung went down on top of Jack. Jack rolled to throw him off— and suddenly there was no more ground beneath them.

"Transmitter is on line, Mr. Pin Wong. Five seconds. And—four—three—two—"

The last second was silent, counted in the head. Then his stage manager pointed at him.

Norman Pin Wong looked directly into the camera and said, "Good day, citizens of the world. I have interrupted your local telecast for an important announcement. My name is Norman Pin Wong. As we begin a new century—not to say a new millennium— we remember that the last century was called 'the American century.' This was due to the fact that America took control of the world. Other countries had controlled large portions of the world in previous centuries, but history passed them by. Other countries attempted to challenge America for control of the world in the twentieth century, but history passed them by as well. America begins this century preeminent. But history is against them." He smiled a slight smile. "*I* am against them."

"Jack should be back by now," said Jennifer. "Shall I go after him?"

"No. He can take care of himself, and I need you with me," said Travis. "It's time to get this show on the road."

Travis and Jen slipped into the rain like ghosts. They had to cross one hundred feet with no other cover, and as luck would have it, the rain grew thicker as they approached the two sentries.

Travis reached out and touched the back of Jen's hand, tapping his fingers on hers. *One—two—* The *three* was silent as they moved forward in unison. Two left hands clamped over the guards' mouths. Two right hands stabbed Tanto knives into throats. The TALON team lowered the bodies silently to the ground, then made their way as quickly as they dared—and sometimes a little *more* quickly as the mud gave way beneath them—one hundred yards down the trail the sentries had guarded, making certain no others were stationed down there.

But they were alone. Somewhere below, a Chinese patrol waited in ambush for the team that would not come. How far below was the question. How soon would they come back once the shooting started up here? Or would they come at all? Maybe they were far enough down that the rain would keep the racket from them. There was no way of telling.

The two went back up the trail, slipping and sliding in the by now well-known red mud. At the top Travis stopped to take three stick grenades from a dead man's rucksack on the ground. He had his own detonation devices but he might as well cache what he could, so he scooped up the ChiCom ordnance and tossed one to Jen. They hurried across the plateau until they came into view of Sam, Sarah, and Iniki. A hand signal said it was time to take the *heiau*.

It would be insane to go in the front door. No matter how easy it looked on television, a man in a doorway is a contained target, and the gray light behind him would make him impossible to miss. Travis waited for Iniki to catch up to him.

"I told you I'd take care of your mountain, but I want to blow the back off *that* place. You gonna give me a hard time?"

"Hell, I was gonna do it myself. The sooner those bastards are out of the *heiau* the better. After Hurricane Iniki, we got used to rebuilding."

Travis unscrewed the metal caps from the hot ends of the handles to uncover the pull rings for the grenades' friction fuzes. He rolled to the back of the building, pulled both rings at once by jamming two fingers through them, and hurled them at the base of the wall before diving to hug the ground.

Norman Pin Wong was in his element. "Around the world, various countries, various factions and groups seek to break free of American influence. Many have formed loose confederations. But they are hampered by their ad hoc nature. I propose to remedy this problem. I shall use my vast resources to establish a central command and focus these entities toward our combined single purpose of eliminating American control.

I shall forge a movement from the billions of non-Americans who seek their own destiny. And I shall begin by devastating the American city of San Diego—"

At that point the wall beyond the camera he was facing exploded.

Chapter 38

Shards of smoking mahogany flew through the air, and one, whirling, caught a Chinese television crewman in his windpipe. He staggered, clawed desperately to get it out—and when he did, it uncorked a gusher of bright red blood. He was dead before he hit the ground.

Travis, Iniki, and Sam were through the hole before the man's body landed. Travis took one look at the television camera and blew it all to hell. TALON Force did not want or need publicity.

The TV crewmen were part of the Triad. They knew how to use weapons but didn't have them handy. That was their mistake. TALON Force blew them all to hell, too.

Norman Pin Wong's hand-picked guards were picking themselves up from the concussion of the blast, dazed but ready to defend their master—when the third ChiCom grenade blew a second hole in the wall behind them. Rain burst into the room along with Jen and Sarah.

With TALON Force members on both sides of the room, it was dangerous for the team to use their XM-29s, so Jennifer took out her Baretta and deftly shot a man at the base of this throat.

A guard went for her, turning his back to Travis.

He yanked out his folding Tanto lock blade and drove it deep into the man's kidneys, then twisted. When he jerked the blade free, it was followed by bright arterial blood.

A third guard lost his head and began spraying the room with lead. But the rain was continuing to blow in, caught in the draft between the two big holes in the *heiau,* and as his AK-47 began to kick it slipped in his hands. He succeeded in cutting one of his own men almost in two before Iniki brought him down with a burst from his XM-29. In the process Iniki accidentally hit another man in the right eye, blowing a gaping hole in the man's skull.

All this had happened in less than thirty seconds—a lifetime for people trained for combat. But Norman Pin Wong had left his combatant days far behind him. It took him the full thirty seconds to adjust to the new realities. He had just been speaking to the world, anointing himself the president of a new world order, on the very verge of killing thousands in San Diego. Now, he was in the middle of a firefight, with rain and bullets whistling past his ears. Miraculously, he was unhurt. His guards were trying to protect him, and the invaders were dealing with them first, ignoring the unarmed man in a two thousand dollar suit. But Norman Pin Wong was far from unarmed.

He dropped to his knees and reached under his shawl-draped chair.

A Chinese raised his AK-47 and snapped off a burst that sailed harmlessly into the rain. Sam pumped two quick shots into the man's chest with his own sidearm, while Jen used hers to spray a long burst across the scene, hearing the bullets hit flesh and mahogany. She dropped to one knee to change the magazine.

"I have Sarin!" shouted Norman Pin Wong. Everyone in the room froze.

The tall, thin man stood holding a metal canister the size of a football.

"I have Sarin," he repeated. "You Americans have

protective suits, but in this gunfire you can't be certain they haven't been breached. You there—look at the rip in your sleeve." He was starting straight at Sarah Greene.

She was staring back, white-lipped.

"My men and I will leave here with that woman as a hostage or I will detonate the gas bomb here and now!"

"You're pretty big on pronouncements," said Sarah softly. "You like the sound of your own voice. What's that you were saying about San Diego?"

"Thank you for reminding me." Norman Pin Wong was smiling, the moment of chaos now passing away. He was in control once more. "I need to alert my pilot to detonate his own bomb before we go."

"Oh no you don't," said Sarah, and put a bullet through the canister.

With a sound like an eighteen-wheeler's hydraulic brakes, the colorless gas inside the canister burst free. Sarah grabbed at her sleeve to hold the rip together. Pin Wong grabbed at his hip where her bullet had lodged—and then Pin Wong and all his men began to spasm as their airways closed and their heads began to pound. One of the guards jerked his trigger finger and put half a magazine into his foot and never noticed.

Travis leapt toward Sarah but found Sam there first. The smallest member of TALON Force pulled her arm against his chest to cover the rip. She turned her head and he was shocked to see her gasping for breath, her dilated pupils locked on his face. "Decon—tamination—" she choked.

Sam threw her face down over his shoulder and staggered out of the *heiau,* into the rain. What had she told them, way back on their first trip across the Pacific to Japan? *"Under wet and humid weather conditions Sarin degrades swiftly. You must decontaminate within one minute."* He lurched away from the building, sideways to the prevailing winds. She was begin-

ning to spasm. *"The most important factor is time."*
He dumped her unceremoniously on the sodden mud
and used his Tanto knife to rip her suit open. The
rain washed over her. He grabbed his decontamination
kit and found the chemical antidote. He dumped it on
her and began to rub it on her arm, then all over her
body. The others were beside him now, helping. Sam
didn't notice.

Chapter 39

In San Diego, all hell had broken loose.

Since Norman Pin Wong's truncated announcement that he meant to decimate this Southern California city, the police, firemen, and troops from the Naval air station were under continuous alert—but no one knew for what. The recent Sarin attacks in Tokyo were fresh in the world's mind, so Sarin was a distinct possibility, but if it were Sarin, where would it be used? San Diego has no subways, and buses or trolleys made little sense. Horton Plaza, the multilevel tourist attraction mall was ordered evacuated, as was the Convention Center, where several thousand comic book enthusiasts were startled to be yanked away from tables filled with super-villain plots for decimating the world. But no one knew what had happened to Norman Pin Wong after the off-stage explosion had startled him so. No one knew when the next shoe would drop.

Including the pilot of UAL 901.

He sat in the cockpit and waited for the signal from Kauai to detonate the plane. He was fully prepared to do so, but he was not prepared to do so without Mr. Pin Wong's order. Mr. Pin Wong had spent his entire career as hidden head of the Ch'u Triad drilling obedience into his underling's heads. As they had proven so often in the past four days, they would do anything for him—once he gave the order. He was a great man; they were his pawns.

Meanwhile, the jetway would be extending into position, and the plane's supposed passengers would be expected to disembark. When they found there was no one on board, the jig would be up.

"UAL nine-oh-one, the jetway is waiting. Please open your hatch."

"Forget that!" Another voice from the control tower blared over the radio. "Do *not* open your hatch! Do you understand me, UAL nine-oh-one? Do *not* open your hatch!"

Did they know? Sweat blistering his brow, the pilot spoke, hoarsely. "I understand, tower. But why?"

"There has been a threat made against the city. We do not yet know its nature but we may ask you to take off again."

This could not be allowed. "I understand, tower, but I am low on fuel. I flew from Hawaii—"

"We know that. Tell us how much fuel you have left and we'll clear a landing within your range. We are currently warning all incoming flights to detour to the five Los Angeles airports."

The jetway bumped against the side of the plane. "I . . . I don't think I should do that . . ."

"Why not?"

"I . . . have a medical emergency. One of my passengers . . . a Mister . . ." Suddenly the pilot's mind went black; he couldn't think of a single name. "A Mister . . ."—*American? 'Merikin?*—". . . Merkin. Mister Merkin. He suffered a heart attack two hours ago."

"You didn't report that, UAL nine-oh-one. When we asked if you had a problem, you said no."

"We have a doctor on board. Two. They had him resting comfortably. It's not an emergency—"

"You just said it was."

"Right. That's right. It wasn't before. But he should

go to a hospital right away now that he's on the ground." *Where was the damn signal??!!!*

"Ask the doctors what supplies they'll need to safeguard him en route to LAX."

The pilot quickly saw that his ruse was not going to work. They were pressing him from all sides. Mr. Pin Wong had clearly announced what would happen to San Diego. Maybe the satellite had been cut off. Maybe the radio signal for this plane had failed. He, the pilot, would be the first to die, and once he was dead it didn't matter what Mr. Pin Wong thought of him. He would have to push the button that would detonate the bomb on his own, and—

"I wouldn't."

A voice from behind! And the cool circle of a gunbarrel pressed to the back of his neck!

No one else was supposed to be on this plane!

The pilot's nerves overcame him. He stabbed frantically at the button with his finger— and then his brains were splattered all across the windshield.

Lieutenant Commander Stan Powczuk, USN, flopped into the co-pilot's chair and passed out.

Chapter 40

In the end, one of Stan's fellow Navy SEALs flew UAL 901 back out to sea, one hundred miles off the coast, and ditched it. He parachuted to a waiting Coast Guard ship, and let the DC-10 find its own way to the water. It arced steeply toward the Pacific and impacted about ten miles away. The impact set off a charge placed in the cockpit to ensure the Sarin bomb detonated. The Sarin would kill fish in the area, and the Coast Guard would make certain the area was off limits for a period of time as a security measure, but the nerve agent would not exist for long underwater.

Meanwhile, Stan was back in the hospital at Coronado Naval Air Station, directly across the bay from San Diego International, being debriefed by Brigadier General Jack Krauss, Task Force Commander.

"You hear me and hear me good, Powczuk! Your country did not create TALON Force so its individual members could nominate themselves for suicide missions. First, you were under orders to recuperate from your chest wound. Second, all TALON members know how much time and effort we put into your operation. My God, man, if any of you were captured and the others weren't dumb enough to climb up a shit hole to rescue them, we would use every available asset to do it. We cannot—*cannot!*—lose you seven.

You're not just the best of our joint services, you're all practically national fucking monuments! And yet there you are, half-dead already, volunteering to infiltrate a plane full of Sarin gas by yourself, without any of the TALON equipment! I've a good mind to toss you back in the drink where I found you!"

"Permission to speak freely, sir?"

"Go ahead."

"Bullshit." Stan grinned up from his hospital bed. "Can I help it if the rest of TALON Force is off on some damn beach in paradise getting a tan? When the chips went down, I had to *represent* the rest of those slackers." Ever since Krauss had shown up on a Navy SEAL training mission in the South Atlantic—"just passing through"—the two of them had enjoyed getting in each other's faces. Stan suspected that Krauss played whatever role the person he wanted to see would best respond to—Sarah had told him the old man had been almost fatherly with her. Well, if butting heads was what he thought Stan liked, he was right, and Stan was happy to oblige him.

"Here I was, following orders, letting a lot of pretty nurses fondle my arm—giving me shots, stroking my chest, changing my bandages. All on account of the Ch'u Triad. And then the whole base goes on disaster alert because some guy on a pirate TV broadcast says he's going to fuck over Sunny D. Well, everybody's immediately thinking Sarin, and I do a little math and ask if any planes have flown in from Hawaii recently. And there's this one that's just landed with a pilot that's acting spooky. So I put on my pants and get some swabby to drive me over to the airport—"

"I'll want that man's name!"

"Yeah, and I want to fuck Michelle Pfeiffer, but that ain't gonna happen either. Sir. So there I am, up in the tower looking at a DC-10 that could be packed full of Sarin, and I'm the only one that's been briefed on the stuff. So I tell 'em to keep the pilot talking and make a little noise at the side hatch while I go down and have a look at the rear hatch. Then when I get inside—"

"You didn't tell the air marshalls anything about going inside!"

"Secrecy, sir. Need to know. I can't tell people I'm a national fucking monument, now can I? So, where was I? Oh yeah, I get inside and every seat in the house has got a canister strapped into it, and we're about a mile and a half from downtown, so I'm figuring everybody from El Cajon to Tijuana dies. At a minimum. Unless I stroll on down and reason with the man with his hand on the button."

"What if just one of those canisters had sprung a leak on its way across the ocean?"

"Well then, the pilot wouldn't be sitting up there trying to bullshit his way through some story about medical emergencies. If he was okay then I was, too. Hell, the Ch'u Triad didn't want their pilots keeling over and parking those canisters in the middle of the Pacific. I bet they did A-number-one work securing them."

"And speaking of medical emergencies," said Krauss, with a glare as cold as at the start of this colloquy, "when the marshalls saw the blood hit the windscreen and followed you inside, they found you out cold."

"Well, you ordered me to rest."

"Powczuk, I have heard some preposterous shit in my time—"

"I bet you have, sir."

"—but that takes the cake. If it were up to me, I'd hang your ass out to dry for about seventeen years. But the president seems to think you did something worthwhile here, so I'm going to let you slide—this time. Still, I don't want you on the same continent with me—and I don't want any reporters tracking down the mystery hero at the airport—so I'm packing your ass back onto another hospital plane and sending you far, far away from here."

"Would that be to Kauai, sir?"

"You're so smart, you tell me."

"I'm sure I could, sir. But actually, I'd appreciate it if you'd tell me what happened with the rest of TALON Force . . ."

Chapter 41

Security was extremely tight around the normally se-
date Wilcox Memorial Hospital, a civilian establishment at the Lihue city limits. Pairs of MPs from the
Pacific Missile Range Facility on the other side of
Kauai stood at each of the entry doors and politely
but thoroughly checked the ID of everyone who came
to go inside. No one on the island could remember
anything like it. It looked like the stories they saw on
CNN about terrorist alerts in Colorado or Florida, but
there were no terrorists on Kauai. There *had* been
that strange disruption in telephone service yesterday,
but the authorities assured everyone that it was just
an unfortunate glitch, and really, this wasn't the mainland, or even Honolulu, where the evils of civilization
lurked. Most likely some visiting dignitary had suffered a heart attack hiking to the Mauna Puluo waterfall on the Na Pali coast, they thought. Tourists really
needed to remember that nature wasn't smoothed
over here.

When Travis, Jennifer, Jack, Sam, and Iniki drove
in Iniki's shiny red Dodge Caravan to the back entrance of Wilcox, they went through the same rigama-
role as everyone else. Then they took the back stairs
to the top floor, where their bona fides were checked

again. Finally, they were admitted to the private ward, occupied by just three patients.

Sarah looked the best of the three. She was weak but the combination of timely decontamination and the pouring rain had removed the Sarin from her body in time. She waved at the visitors when they came in, and happily accepted the vases of flowers both Sam and Iniki had brought her. Secretly, she was thrilled by Sam's gift because it contained the rarest orchids the island could provide, and she knew he'd searched them out especially for her, but she made sure to act just as effusive over Iniki's more standard bouquet.

Stan looked the worst of them. They had all heard about his heroics in San Diego, and the tongue-lashing from TALON Force command, and the long flight from Taiwan to California plus the flight from California to Kauai had added to the cost. He immediately started bitching that he didn't belong here, but no one came close to believing him.

Finally, there was Hunter. By the time Air-Sea Rescue had found him, he had been well on his way toward hypothermia, but ASR were old hands at treating that specific ailment and had him wrapped in aluminum blankets the moment he was lifted into their chopper. Once at Wilcox, he immediately started bitching about having to share a room with Stan.

"But at least I got to hear about your adventures on Waialeale," he added. "I don't know which I'm happier I missed, the forced march up the mountain or the dash back down carrying Sarah."

"I'm just as happy I missed that part," Sarah replied. "It would have scared me shitless. Going up you were only going to fall five or six feet forward. Going down you could slide down whole hillsides."

"Tell me about it," said Jack. "When Pin Wong's technician took me off the edge, we dropped a good twenty feet before we hit the slope, and rolled another hundred, at least. Naturally, I made sure he was under me when we hit, and since that knocked all the air out of him I was able to hold him in front of me as we rolled, but you know what they say—it's not the fall, it's the sudden stop. When we hit some big damn tree we were sideways. I must have been out for a good five minutes, and it's just luck I didn't drown in that monsoon. Of course my pal died of a broken spine and a punctured lung. But by the time I got back up the hill and to the *heiau,* I'd missed all the fun. Except for Sam ripping off Sarah's clothes, of course."

"If only," mumbled Sam, blushing to the roots of his hair.

"Well, I fell thirty thousand feet," said Hunter, "so don't go whining over a hundred and twenty. But I had a chute . . . unlike those poor bastards on the San Diego flight."

"Judging from your report, I don't see how you could have done any more than you did," said Travis.

"Yeah, that's right, keep the patient's spirits up," answered Hunter. "But if I didn't bring both planes down, I didn't do the job."

"Fuck you," said Stan. "If you'd brought them both down I wouldn't have been able to be a hero. You're just tryin' to steal my thunder, rich boy."

"Big words from a pygmy."

"You want me to come over there and pound your face in?"

"You can't reach my face."

"All right, knock it off," said Travis. "This is still a team, even if half of us are stuck here for the duration."

"What I don't understand—if I may," said Iniki, "is why you shot Pin Wong, Sarah. Knowing your suit was ripped, I mean."

"TALON Force is why," she said. "It's why I joined it—to take out of the world people who do things as horrible as using Sarin gas on an innocent populace. And if I died destroying him, then I died for the very reason I was standing on that mountaintop—in that sacred space." Her smile wrinkled her perky nose. "But I'd told my team what to do, and I knew they'd do it. So I really wasn't in any danger at all."

Iniki snapped off a salute to Sarah. "To the bravest warrior I have ever known," he said.

He looked around at the others in turn. "Stan—Hunter—Jen—Jack—Sam—Travis. The bravest *team* I've ever known. None of you has forgotten what it means to be alive. Not even you, Jack," he said, grinning.

"*Especially* not me," Jack grinned back.

Iniki turned to Travis. "Major Barrett, if your team ever needs a replacement, which judging from this room means next Thursday, I would be honored to be considered. But in the meantime, I wish you a pleasant time on my island. When everyone's fully recovered—and assuming you haven't blasted out of here to go deal with some other situation someplace else in the world—I will throw you a luau to end all luaus. I happen to know a sacred place, on a beautiful beach you get to by Hawaiian War Canoe . . . just like in the guide books . . ."

"Stop it, Iniki," said Hunter. "You're killing me!"

"C'mon, people. Let's let these three get some rest," said Travis. The visitors turned to go.

"Enjoy your flowers, Sarah," Sam said. It was a casual enough statement, but something in his voice caught her attention. She looked up and he was watching her with something between friendship and intensity. Then he turned and left with the others.

She looked down at her flowers and spotted a small piece of paper thrust among the irises. She pulled it free and read it.

Sarah,
I finally traced the message back from the NSA. Switzerland to Liberia to Canada—and then to Norway. The home of a Doctor Olaf Magnuson—a name you once mentioned to me from your last time in

Tokyo. The final leg to the Amazon was easy, after that.

I imagine Dr. Magnuson has kept his ties to the Tokyo medical establishment, and to you. I believe he was alerted to the attack by his friends, and he alerted you—and you then routed a message back across the world to bring TALON Force into a situation it wasn't tasked to confront.

I imagine, I believe . . . and I know how much Sarin and Tokyo mean to you. So I'll tell the boss I couldn't get to the source, and hope he never finds out. But please, Sarah—don't do it again. I'm not afraid of Sarin, but Travis sure makes me sweat.

Your friend,
Sam